P9-CRX-263

"What are you doing here, Honor?" Johnny asked, catching her by the wrist. "What are you trying to do to me?"

"I wasn't thinking straight," she implored softly. "Let me go and—"

He imprisoned both her wrists in one hand and brought her closer to him. "What were you thinking, coming up here? Don't you know what I could do to you? Don't you know what I *want* to do to you?"

She trembled, but lifted her chin and said, "Yes . . . I know."

But she didn't know. She thought he meant sex, and he did, of course. He wanted to take her every way a man could take a woman, wanted it so badly it hurt. But sex wasn't enough. He needed justice. Her tears for his.

"Johnny, I never meant to hurt you," she whispered.

He gripped her shoulders and brought her to his mouth, hissing out his pent-up fury, whispering of her betrayal, shuddering with naked longing as their lips touched. . . .

WHAT ARE *LOVESWEPT* ROMANCES?

They are stories of true romance and touching emotion. We believe those two very important ingredients are constants in our highly sensual and very believable stories in the *LOVESWEPT* line. Our goal is to give you, the reader, stories of consistently high quality that may sometimes make you laugh, sometimes make you cry, but are always fresh and creative and contain many delightful surprises within their pages.

Most romance fans read an enormous number of books. Those they truly love, they keep. Others may be traded with friends and soon forgotten. We hope that each *LOVESWEPT* romance will be a treasure—a "keeper." We will always try to publish

*LOVE STORIES YOU'LL NEVER FORGET
BY AUTHORS YOU'LL ALWAYS REMEMBER*

The Editors

Loveswept® 581

Suzanne Forster
Night of the Panther

BANTAM BOOKS
NEW YORK · TORONTO · LONDON · SYDNEY · AUCKLAND

NIGHT OF THE PANTHER

A Bantam Book / November 1992

LOVESWEPT® and the wave design are registered
trademarks of Bantam Books, a division of
Bantam Doubleday Dell Publishing Group, Inc.
Registered in U.S. Patent
and Trademark Office and elsewhere.

All rights reserved.
Copyright © 1992 by Suzanne Forster.
Cover art copyright © 1992 by Peter Attard.
No part of this book may be reproduced or transmitted
in any form or by any means, electronic or mechanical,
including photocopying, recording, or by any
information storage and retrieval system, without
permission in writing from the publisher.
For information address: Bantam Books.

If you purchased this book without a cover you should be
aware that this book is stolen property. It was reported as
"unsold and destroyed" to the publisher and neither the
author nor the publisher has received any payment for this
"stripped book."

If you would be interested in receiving protective vinyl
covers for your Loveswept books, please write to this address
for information:

Loveswept
Bantam Books
P.O. Box 985
Hicksville, NY 11802

ISBN 0-553-44216-3

Published simultaneously in the United States and Canada

Bantam Books are published by Bantam Books, a division of
Bantam Doubleday Dell Publishing Group, Inc. Its trademark,
consisting of the words "Bantam Books" and the portrayal of
a rooster, is Registered in U.S. Patent and Trademark Office
and in other countries. Marca Registrada. Bantam Books, 666
Fifth Avenue, New York, New York 10103.

PRINTED IN THE UNITED STATES OF AMERICA

OPM   0 9 8 7 6 5 4 3 2 1

Acknowledgments

Many thanks to John Flint, a volunteer at the Apache Culture Center in Fort Apache, Arizona, for taking the time to describe the natural beauty of the White Mountain Apache Reservation to me, complete with the technical logistics of the town of Whiteriver. He was infinitely patient with a nervous writer who'd never personally visited the reservation but wanted very much to get the details right. If I succeeded, he deserves a large share of the credit. Where I didn't succeed, the responsibility is entirely mine.

My thanks also to Edgar Perry, head of the Apache Culture Center, for the graciousness with which he allowed me to interrupt his busy schedule with my questions. I owe a debt of gratitude to both Mr. Perry and Mr. Flint for their input on ancient Apache rituals and ceremonies—and for understanding that I had to take some "literary license" with certain elements of a rich and wonderful culture for the dramatic purposes of this story.

Prologue

A savage war cry shattered the night.

Out of the blackwashed hills came a phantom on horseback, a rider as naked as his lunging stallion. His spear was tipped with blood, and his dark eyes were wild with triumph. The enemy was vanquished. He had won the fight for his life, for his sovereign soul. The great bear was dead.

An aura of strange light spilled over him as he raised his weapon to the hunter's moon and howled like a wolf. A lone white hawk joined the cry, screaming as it swooped overhead. The warrior watched the bird soar and dip, its pale wings flashing silver in the icy moonlight. Struck by the creature's haunting beauty, the warrior knew he had to have it. The white hawk was a prize that would make him the most powerful among his people.

He followed the bird's flight on horseback, mesmerized by its glow as it glided toward the branches of a tree. The limb it settled on overhung a thunderous river. Majestic and solemn, the bird was silent and still as it watched the warrior pull an arrow from his quiver.

The bow vibrated in the warrior's grip as he drew back the arrow. The bird's sad gaze bore down on him, mystifying him. He could almost feel the creature's mournful plea for forgiveness, its mute acceptance of the inevitable.

The hawk was sacrificing itself, he realized.

The warrior's hand shook. A film of cold sweat coated his body, but the hunting instinct was too strong, too ancient, to be controlled. His muscles worked of their own will, straining for the last ounce of force, inching the arrow back.

As the missile struck its target, the warrior was stabbed with unbearable pain. His field of vision blurred as the wounded hawk unfurled its wings, creating a magnificent cape of white, then transformed before his eyes into a hauntingly beautiful woman. The cape fell away, and long golden hair flew around her, exposing her nakedness. A look of anguish clouded her exquisite eyes.

She was bleeding, he realized. The arrow had pierced her heart, and the life force was ebbing from her in a bright crimson ribbon. She was dying. Heat seared his chest as if the arrow had struck him.

She tumbled from the branch into the water and disappeared in its turbulent depths. The warrior froze in motion. She had fallen into the river of memory. He couldn't follow her there without drowning in his own past, in his own rage and despair.

"Johnny . . . forgive me!"

The anguished cry rose out of nowhere. It dragged him to the water's edge where he could see her silvery form in the murky depths. Heedless of the river's curse, he plunged into the water. . . .

The old man opened his eyes slowly, the flame of the crackling bonfire reflected in his trancelike gaze. He had been fasting for days, seeking wisdom. The dream had shown him what he must do. He had to find her, the woman with sunlight for hair and rainwater for eyes. *The woman who had betrayed Johnny.* She was the only one who could bring him back.

One

Johnny Starhawk was the one they'd all come to see.

The courtroom was packed to capacity with concerned citizens and curious spectators. Young lawyers squeezed together to catch a glimpse of the "renegade with a cause" in action. Outside, in the halls, the media waited, ready to pounce on the Irish-Apache attorney when the legal proceedings broke. The trial was a hotly contested one, a contract dispute between a small community church and a huge multinational oil company.

Starhawk was defending the church's right to lease oil-company land, and he was arguably the most controversial, yet celebrated, attorney in the country at the moment. His recent victories in civil-rights and environmental law had made him a legend at thirty-five. Everyone wanted a piece of him. Nobody really knew him . . . with the exception of a quietly beautiful young woman sitting unnoticed in the back of the spectators' gallery.

Honor Bartholomew had taken a seat there, hoping not to be seen. To that end, she had dressed in nondescript gray clothes, and covered with a scarf the long blond hair she'd knotted in a loose coil at the back of her neck. But it was Starhawk's notice she feared, not the media's.

Clutching a small turquoise stone in her hand, she kept a watchful eye on Starhawk, whose back was to her, his exotic black hair spilling over his shoulders as he sat at the defendant's table and jotted notes. The stone grew warm as Honor worked its smoothness between her fingers.

Johnny Starhawk had given her the Apache good-luck charm a very long time ago, just days before another trial took place. Only Johnny wasn't an attorney then; he was the sixteen-year-old defendant, and the trial's tragic outcome had altered the course of both their young lives. That was eighteen years ago, and Honor hadn't seen Johnny since . . . until today.

The question that tormented her now was why she was here, sitting in a courtroom in Washington, D.C., over a thousand miles from home. It had been an impulsive, emotional decision. She'd come at the behest of Johnny's maternal grandfather, an uncanny old man with rattlesnake eyes who called himself Chy Starhawk. The Apache shaman had shown up in her Scottsdale, Arizona, bookstore a week ago with a bizarre request for help that had truly astonished her.

"Only you can bring Johnny Starhawk back to the white mountains," he'd told her, transfixing her with his strange, lidless gaze. "Go to him," he'd urged her quietly. "He will come back for you."

At the mention of Johnny Starhawk's name after so many years, Honor had been stunned and disbelieving. She'd had no idea what the old man was talking about or why it was so important that Johnny return to his tribe until the shaman began to describe the terrible setbacks on the White Mountain Apache Reservation. The tribe's livelihood was in jeopardy, he'd explained. Its cattle were sick, dying. Pollution from a nearby uranium mine was fouling the streams and rivers, but the Apache hadn't been able to get an injunction against the mining company.

Honor had known immediately that he was talking about her father's mine. She'd been estranged from Hale Bartholomew for years, but she was well aware of her father's bottom-line attitude toward environmental concerns. He'd always maintained that saving jobs was more important than saving trees. Even as a child, Honor had seen both sides of the argument, but she'd known better than to clash with her formidable father.

"What you're asking is impossible," she'd told the shaman. "If Johnny remembers me at all, it's not with goodwill. He must still . . . hate me. Surely you know that."

"I know only what the dreams tell me," the old man had countered. "My grandson vowed never to return when he left the reservation. He won't come back for me, but he will for you."

His certainty had been hypnotic. Honor had found herself being drawn in, swayed by him, especially since she was sympathetic to the tribe's plight. But somehow she'd resisted Chy Starhawk, even when he'd vividly described his prophetic dreams and his belief that only Johnny could win a lawsuit against the mining company. She'd had to resist him. He'd said nothing to ease her fears about Johnny's hatred. "I'm not the right person," she told him.

"You are." The old man's voice was firm, as if there were no doubt of it. "And you will go. Not for me, or even for the White Mountain Apache. You will do it for yourself. It's the only way you can be free of the past."

Honor had recoiled from the cold truth of that statement. It had rocked her to have her past sins thrown up to her so unexpectedly. But in the end she'd known he was right. She had never been free from guilt in the eighteen years since she'd last seen

Johnny. She was the reason he'd been sent away. She was the one who had betrayed him. . . .

"Do you believe in a higher power, Mr. Rutledge?" Johnny's voice brought Honor back to the present. He had risen to cross-examine a witness for the plaintiff, one of the oil company's executives, but Honor was barely aware of the man's awkward attempts to answer the question. Her attention was riveted on Johnny. She was hungry for whatever information her senses could give her about him. She needed to know how he might have changed. And she was praying that he hadn't.

She'd followed his career through newspaper and magazine accounts, and she was familiar with the media's fascination with his "pantherish charisma" and his "killer instincts." They questioned him at press conferences about his predatory style, and interviewed him on issue-oriented talk shows about his views. But whether they agreed or disagreed with his latest cause, they flocked to his trials to watch the panther make his next kill.

Their references weren't wasted on him, Honor conceded silently. Defying courtroom tradition, Johnny wore his jet-black hair long and free-flowing, as much a symbol of power as any animal's mane in the wild. Even his eyes lent themselves to the imagery. They flashed like mercury when the light struck them, reminding her of a cat's opaque glare. Maturity had given him height and muscularity, she acknowledged silently. It had made him physically powerful, but it had taken nothing away from his lethal grace.

"Would you have the church demolished, Mr. Rutledge?" Johnny asked, quietly cornering the executive. "And then what? You'd build a gas station in its place? Or a storage yard?"

He allowed the man to fumble overlong with his answer before posing another, equally damaging question. "Or maybe you'd sell the land to the highest bidder? Its market value has appreciated considerably in the twenty years since the church was built, hasn't it?"

Over the next quarter hour Johnny continued to stalk the flustered executive, flushing out his moral ambiguities with the stealth and cunning of a natural predator.

He had changed, Honor realized, bringing the stone to her lips as she sensed how much. The fiery pride she remembered was still there, evident in the taut slash of muscle that rode his jawline. But it was fueled by a new, more potent weapon—ruthlessness. She could see the cold calculation at work in his eyes, the native intelligence. Like a cat, he was infinitely patient with his prey. And like a cat, merciless.

"What is the value of a small community church?" Johnny asked, posing the question to the executive as he turned to the gallery, his dark gaze sweeping the room. Honor pressed her back against the wooden bench, afraid he might see her. But his eyes passed over her without any sign of recognition.

Her heart was pounding wildly. Once she'd decided to make the trip, she'd convinced herself that if she could watch him work, she would be better prepared to deal with him in person. She couldn't have been more wrong. After observing his performance today, the prospect of coming face-to-face with him terrified her. The press was right. He did have killer instincts. His prowess in the courtroom lent him an aspect of danger and unpredictability, of deadly advantage.

And yet she had no choice in the matter. She had an appointment the next morning. She'd made arrangements with his secretary to see him at ten, and so far the appointment hadn't been canceled, even though she'd used her own name. It had surprised her that he would be willing to see her. Was it possible he didn't remember her? It had been so many years.

Her thoughts drifted automatically to the only other time she'd seen him in a courtroom. She'd been called at the last minute by the prosecution as a surprise witness. Johnny had been charged with three counts of assault and battery against high school boys his own age. She'd fought against testifying, pleading with her father not to make her take the stand; but he'd been unrelenting, and finally he'd persuaded her it was the right thing to do. To her eternal regret, she had believed him.

She would never forget the confusion in Johnny's expression as her name was called, and she walked to the front of the courtroom, tears in her eyes. By the time she'd told the prosecutor what she knew, Johnny's confusion was gone, replaced by pain and rage. It was her testimony that had convicted him.

Honor adjusted the gold bracelet band of her wristwatch, opening and refastening a clasp she knew was already secure. It was now thirty minutes past her scheduled appointment time with Johnny, and it wouldn't have surprised her if he was intentionally keeping her waiting. If he'd hoped to make her nervous, it was working. The minutes were ticking away in her head like a countdown to Judgment Day.

She'd taken in every detail of his beautiful but severely appointed reception room—from the neo-modern decor and the striking black-and-white photographs hanging on the walls to the sleek thirtyish receptionist who'd greeted her without the slightest hint of curiosity.

Honor had even taken inventory of her own clothing, wondering if the sandwashed silk suit she wore was appropriate. Were its dusty pink hues too pale for her fair skin? The shawl collar overly feminine?

As she tucked an errant strand of blond hair into the softly braided coil at the nape of her neck, she glanced up at Johnny's office door. The dark wooden portal was a compelling trigger to her deeper fears. Her mind made a startling leap ahead, trying to predict the future, imagining what consequences awaited her on the other side.

How would he react to seeing her after all these years? If she'd been dealing with any other man, she might have been able to convince herself that years could make a difference, that time had worked its own healing process. But she'd seen him in the courtroom; she'd watched his skill at using the witness's weaknesses against him. He'd been unrelenting.

She knew in her heart that if Johnny Starhawk was the kind of man who sought revenge, she would be all but helpless against him. It wasn't just the guilt she harbored. She was not a fighter by nature. She didn't have the instinct for it. He did. It came to him through ancient bloodlines. She could remember reading historical references about travelers who reserved the last shot in their revolvers for their own heads if they were captured by Apaches, so excruciating were the tribe's methods of torture thought to be.

Honor pulled a magazine from the table in front of her and chided herself for being an alarmist. She didn't need Johnny to scare her; she was doing a fine job of that herself.

"Ms. Bartholomew? Mr. Starhawk will see you now."

The magazine slipped from Honor's hands. She rose, unbearably nervous.

He was standing by the window, seemingly unaware of her as she entered his spacious office. His profile tugged cruelly at her emotions. There were things about him that hadn't changed, things that would never change—from the high arc of his cheekbones to his fine, sensual mouth. The promise of male beauty in his youth was stunningly realized in his dark and brooding features.

But it was the shadowed melancholy in his expression that caught at her heart. It dragged her back eighteen years, bringing home a painful awareness. This imposing man was once the sad and lonely boy she'd known.

For a moment she forgot to be cautious. She wanted to walk over and touch his arm, to be whisked back in time to the river where they used to meet, to see his dark eyes regarding her with silent wonder. It astonished her now to remember how much she'd loved that lithe, dusky-skinned boy. No one had reached inside her silence but Johnny, no one had touched her heart and brought her out but him. . . .

She said his name, whispered it softly.

He inhaled sharply, and she thought she heard his breath tremble as he released it. But when he turned toward her, and she caught the icy glint of his eyes, she knew she was wrong. Johnny Starhawk, the man, had no melancholy left in him, no sad emotions where she was concerned. Only coldness.

"To what do I owe the . . . honor?" he asked. The edge he put on her name was cruel.

"I'm here to—" She broke off, sensing the futility of appealing to his sympathies in any way. "I was in the area, and I thought—"

"In the area?" He cut her off softly, savagely. "Don't patronize me, Honor. And don't waste both our time. Just tell me what you're doing here."

She stepped back, frightened. "All right then. I'm here to ask for your help, that's all. But it's important."

He approached the desk, a faint smile compressing his lips. "My help?" he said, taking in her clothing, hair, and jewelry as though they were incriminating evidence of a plot to exploit the masses. Even as a young girl, she'd sensed his unspoken disapproval of her family's wealth, and yet now, from all appearances, he'd gone to great lengths to surround himself with expensive trappings.

"I'm not asking for myself," she said.

"Ah, that explains it." He flashed a quick, cold smile. "Slumming, are we? Got some worthy cause you want the courtroom warrior to promote now that he's made a name for himself? Maybe I could be your poster boy?"

Honor steeled herself against his cutting tone. His ability to slice to the bone with words had always intimidated her. But at least he'd made clear the rules of this game they were about to play. The gloves were off. He meant things to be nasty. Still, she realized, for all his apparent desire to wound her, there was something fiendishly beautiful about his wrath, and she, after all, was a deserving target.

He nodded toward one of the chairs that faced his desk.

She took it, relieved when he sat down as well. Somehow he didn't seem quite so dangerous across the expanse of teakwood, perhaps because their heights were more equal. She gauged him to be at least six foot two, several inches taller than she was at five foot five.

"I wasn't sure you'd remember me," she said, making a clumsy attempt at conversation. "It's been a long time."

The bones of his face seemed to sharpen as he stared at her, intensifying the dark, flaring angles. "You don't give yourself enough credit," he said. "I've been trying to forget you for eighteen years."

Honor touched the hem of her jacket with unsteady fingers, adjusting the silky material. She'd opened herself for that blow. What she hadn't expected was that he would so readily admit how affected he'd been by her.

She glanced up, wishing she could express to him how sorry she was, longing to say anything that would help heal the wounds. But even if she'd been able to summon the words, it wouldn't have been safe to utter them. The cold white flame that burned in his eyes told her not to try anything so condescending as an apology after all this time.

"Maybe I should tell you why I'm here," she suggested.

"Yes." He leaned back in the leather executive chair, ebony hair cascading down his back. "Do that."

"I'm sure you're aware of what's happening on the White Mountain Reservation." She hesitated, anticipating a reaction, and got none. "They believe something's polluting the groundwater."

"What does that have to do with you? Or me?"

Honor saw no choice but to tell him what had happened. It was the only way to explain why she was there. The shaman had told her that he'd called and written Johnny, asking for help, but Johnny had turned down his requests. Obviously the old man intended Honor to be a troubleshooter. She'd been sent in to fix a problem no one else could.

"Your grandfather came to my bookstore in Scottsdale," she explained. "He asked if I would talk to you."

"He came to you? Why?"

"Perhaps because of my father," she said, sensing that now wasn't the time to reveal Chy Starhawk's real reasons. "They say it's runoff from the Bartholomew mines that's fouling the pastureland water."

Johnny didn't respond except to tilt back and rest his head against the chair as he studied her. *Tough break, but it's not my problem,* he seemed to be saying.

"I know you're not on the best of terms with your grandfather," Honor continued, goaded by his silence. "But isn't there something you can do? The tribe's livelihood is at stake."

The light caught his hair, giving it an iridescent sheen as he swung around in the chair and stared out the window. "I did do something," he said. "I wrote the tribal council and offered to send someone in my place, one of my colleagues. He's a bright young lawyer, familiar with both environmental and tribal law." He turned back from the window. "My grandfather refused."

Honor wasn't surprised. The shaman hadn't mentioned Johnny's counteroffer, but Honor knew a substitute would never satisfy the old man. The warrior he'd seen in his dream had been his grandson.

Honor considered telling Johnny what she knew of the dream, hoping it would help him understand his grandfather's urgency. Her only hesitation came from knowing about the dark prophecy associated with Johnny's origins. There was bad blood between Johnny and Chy Starhawk.

Months before Johnny's birth, the shaman had had another dream, one that foretold tragedy. Johnny's mother had become pregnant by an Irish artisan with whom she was desperately in love. But the man didn't share her feelings, and when he abandoned her, she became despondent. Two days after Johnny's birth, she drowned herself in a river that ran through the reservation. Her suicide seemed to fulfill the dark prophecy, and Johnny had never been able to escape it. It had caused him to be shunned by those in his tribe who still believed in the ancient ways. It had made him an outsider among his own people.

"Why are you here, Honor?"

Johnny's question startled her. "I thought I told you," she said. "Your grandfather asked me to come, and I felt . . . an obligation."

"An obligation? In what way?"

The hooded interest in his eyes made her cautious.

If he'd been at all receptive or compassionate, she might have told him that she was there because of him, that she was trying to atone in this way for her part in what had happened. It would have been such a relief to unburden herself of the guilt she'd lived with, to share the heartache. All she'd ever wanted was his forgiveness.

But she couldn't open herself up that way. Everything about him seemed poised for some retaliatory move. She was aware of the flicker of alertness in his gaze, the glare of rapidly contracting pupils. He had the instincts of a hunting cat, and he was waiting for her to reveal herself, to give him a fatal glimpse of her vulnerability.

"If the Bartholomew mines are involved," she said finally, "then I have a responsibility to try to help."

He remained tilted back in the chair, contemplating her. "I'm surprised at you, Honor," he said, his voice dangerously soft. "I never thought you'd go up against your father this way. But then betrayal comes naturally to you, doesn't it?"

Honor bit back a stunned gasp. Did he hate her so much? "That's unfair," she said, her voice shaking. "My father and I haven't spoken in years. I could hardly bear the sight of him after your trial. He—"

She broke off, wanting desperately to put the blame for what happened on her father, yet knowing she couldn't, not totally. He had put terrible pressure on her. He'd made promises he didn't keep, but she was the one who'd taken the witness stand. She was the one who'd testified.

"My relationship with him has deteriorated completely," she said, her voice flattened by the weight of despair she felt. "I left home after college. I haven't seen him since."

Johnny rose abruptly and walked to the window, staring out. He was a formidable figure in the streaming light, icy and remote, his jaw tautly flexed.

Honor drew in a breath, gathering herself, trying to remember what she was there for. "I didn't come here to drag up the past," she said. "And even if I had, it's clear that the last thing you want to hear from me is how sorry I am. But I am sorry—" She caught back a sob, startled at the raw pain locked up in that one word. "*Terribly*. Now . . . please, couldn't we put our differences aside for a moment and talk about the reservation?"

He remained at the window, his gaze fixed on some distant point. "Go ahead," he said after a moment. "Talk. Apparently that's what you came here for."

His supreme indifference in the face of her pain angered her. She found herself wanting to say something that would shake him up, force him to respond. Anything was better than his glacial contempt. "Those mountains were your home once," she said hotly. "Is all that gone, your sense of community, of belonging? And if you don't care about the people, what about the animals and the trees? I can't believe you want to see all that natural beauty destroyed, contaminated with toxic runoff and chemical sludge."

He sighed wearily, impatient with it all. "Aren't you getting carried away, Honor? The tribe has access to lawyers from the Indian Legal Services. The offer of my colleague is still good if they want it. They'll be fine."

She rose out of the chair. "But, Johnny, they want you! You're one of them, for God's sake. Have you forgotten you're half-Apache?"

He whirled on her, the icy flame leaping in his eyes. "Forgotten?" he said. "I wish to hell I *could* forget. What would you like me to remember about my Apache heritage, Honor? That my warrior ancestors believed in retribution? That vengeance was a matter of honor? An Apache never forgets a betrayal, *never forgives*. Is that what you want me to remember?"

She stepped back, trembling. His body was taut,

poised to strike, alive with uncoiling threat. She had always known in her soul that if something turned Johnny Starhawk cold, he would be a dangerous man.

"Get out of here, Honor," he said harshly. "Make a run for it now, while I'm still feeling civilized enough to let you go."

Two

Alone in his office, Johnny was grimly aware of his own raging pulse. It had been eighteen years since he'd seen her, but she hadn't changed. She still had that same hesitant, maybe-we-could-be-friends smile he'd found irresistible when they were teenagers. She was still golden, still as pristine and untouchable as he remembered. And God, achingly beautiful with all that trembling anguish in her voice. Even when she was trying to be tough, her blue-gray gaze was wistful, pleading to be understood.

He swept a hand through his hair, shoving back the darkness that had fallen over his eyes as he stared at the door she'd just fled through. He thought he'd conquered his feelings for her. He'd thought himself free, but perhaps he would never be free of her. From the first moment he'd set eyes on her in the dingy corridors of Roosevelt High School so many years ago, he'd known she was *boo begoz'aa da*, forbidden to him.

Her father's wealth and position alone made her unreachable, but something far more basic than that had kept him at a distance—her pale beauty. Her eyes were the same color as the morning mists that rose off the river bordering her family's estate, separating it from the reservation. He'd noticed her walking there, a pensive dreamer, haunting the opposite shore. She'd had a translucent quality he associated with fragile things, rose petals and dragonfly wings. A hard touch—a man's touch—would surely leave marks on her body. At sixteen that thought had both aroused and frightened him.

He might never have spoken to her at all if she hadn't broken the barriers with her shy smile. He'd noticed her glancing at him when they passed in the hallways at high school. But when he'd turned, she was always too far away, darting in and out of his focus like a deer seen through rifle sights. Finally one day, his curiosity aroused, he'd followed her to her locker. He was standing across the narrow corridor, waiting when she turned. There was nowhere for her to run, nowhere to hide, and after a moment of visible panic, she'd found her smile again.

A shaking sound had trembled on her lips as he'd approached, half whimper, half sigh. It had astonished him, that sound. It had ripped through his heart and gut, turning him into a hardened animal. All he'd wanted was to touch her. His body spasmed painfully with the impulse, but his hand had locked. He couldn't do it. Something powerful had held him back, something as ancient and unchangeable as his Apache bloodlines.

That first encounter had set the boundaries of their relationship. They were destined to become friends, kindred spirits, to share their loneliness, but nothing else. He had never touched her in all the months they knew each other, except accidentally once, and even then the sight of his dark hand on her fair skin had made them both pull back. Their eyes had met, and the staggering sexual truth of their attraction couldn't be denied.

They had never touched again.

Johnny's hand clenched painfully now as he remembered the rest. He'd fought the young toughs who'd taunted and humiliated her, almost killing one of them. He'd protected Honor Bartholomew from everything and everyone, especially from himself.

He dragged back his chair and sank down in it, sweeping a hand across his desk as if to clear the clutter. A pencil box and letter opener went flying. Close up the wound, Starhawk, he told himself savagely. You're bleeding all over the place. It was insane to let himself wallow in romantic teenage swill this way. He had work to do, a landmark case in progress. She'd disrupted his schedule enough for one day. Make that one lifetime, he thought.

He glanced at his desk calender and saw Honor's name in the ten o'clock slot, neatly printed by his secretary. The pain that rose inside him was lacerating as he pulled the page from its binding and crushed it in his fist. Seeing her again had brought it all back. Now even to read her name ripped at him.

For all the anguish in her eyes, she couldn't possibly have been torn apart the way he had. Every barely audible word she'd uttered on that witness stand had clawed a piece from his soul. Just once, he thought. Just once I want her to know this pain, to hurt the way I have.

"Pack your clothes, lady! Go home."

Honor sighed heavily. She'd been issuing that order to herself all evening, but she hadn't yet moved from where she sat in the wingback chair of her hotel room. Not even to seek sustenance or to answer nature's call. She couldn't. She was immobilized, like a woman turned to stone. Not that she questioned the soundness of her own advice. It was probably the sanest plan she'd had in recent days, but something wouldn't let her act on it.

"Leave now," she promised herself, "and this is the worst it will get. You'll go back to Scottsdale, reopen your bookstore, and all this will seem like a bad dream."

She pressed her fingers to her temples, massaging the hot throb that wouldn't go away. The worst was plenty bad enough. She had a headache coming on, and her whole body felt bruised and aching. However, if she stayed, a headache would be the least of her worries. Johnny seemed determined to wreak havoc, and vengeance, and anything else that could possibly be wreaked. It was a frightening prospect.

"Go *home*, Honor. Pack. Get on that plane." She glanced over at her suitcase and felt the impulse to act move through her, but she couldn't make herself do it. Going home was too easy. There were any number of reasons why she couldn't board that plane and fly away with a clear conscience.

She'd be letting Chy Starhawk down, but perhaps more important, she'd be letting herself down. Going home was exactly what Johnny would expect her to do. He undoubtedly thought of her as weak-willed, and she couldn't fault him for that. He had little reason to think otherwise.

She'd let herself be swayed by her father, admittedly an intimidating man for a fourteen-year-old to defy, and the results had been disastrous. He'd persuaded her that if she didn't testify voluntarily, she would be subpoenaed, which would reflect badly on the Bartholomew name. And then he'd promised to intervene with the judge, an old friend, if Johnny was convicted, and see that Johnny didn't serve any time. Afterward she'd realized his plan all along was to separate her and Johnny.

After the trial, when she'd gone to see Johnny to beg his forgiveness and try to explain, she'd learned he'd been sent away as a condition of his suspended sentence. She'd been talked out of trying to find him by his Apache godmother, the woman who'd raised him after his own mother died. A petite, soft-spoken woman, his godmother had been both compassionate and convincing as she begged Honor to leave Johnny alone, to let him get on with his life and make whatever he could of it. He'd been hurt enough, she'd said.

Honor had been a shy child by nature and raised to be mindful of authority and respectfully obedient to the adults in her life. Spontaneity was not encouraged, and what independent spirit stirred inside her gentle soul was quickly squashed under the weight of her father's rules and regulations.

But she was an adult now. Whether it was fate or circumstance that had intervened in the form of Johnny's grandfather, he was giving her an opportunity to right a wrong, and this time she needed to follow through, to have the courage of her conscience. She had something to prove, to herself as well as Johnny.

She rose from the chair and released a sigh of relief. Free at last! An uneasy smile crossed her face as she glanced at her reflection in the dresser's mirror. But free for what? A fight to the death with the courtroom warrior?

Good manners are never old-fashioned. It was her mother's favorite saying, and Honor could almost hear Adele Bartholomew's musical tones resonating in her head as she smiled politely at one of the most obstinate women she had ever encountered, Johnny Starhawk's receptionist.

"If you won't make me an appointment," Honor said, "then perhaps you'll tell me when Mr. Starhawk is coming in?"

The svelte auburn-haired receptionist shot Honor a glare designed to vaporize her on the spot. "Mr. Starhawk isn't coming in this morning," she said, turning back to her typewriter. "He's in court."

"In that case," Honor said evenly, "I'll wait."

The secretary drew a deep breath and mustered a

cold smile. "I think Mr. Starhawk would prefer that you *didn't*."

The gauntlet had been thrown down. "I'd prefer to hear that from Mr. Starhawk himself, thank you," Honor said politely but firmly.

"You're about to get your wish."

The deep tone of Johnny's words sent a shock wave of alarm through Honor. It had come from behind her, but she hadn't even heard the office door open. When had he entered the room?

She whirled to face him and saw the menace in his dark eyes even before he voiced it. "If you know what's good for you"—he said so softly he could barely be heard—"you'll get the hell out of here."

Honor tried to speak, but she was trembling too hard. A shudder of fear weakened her thighs and swept up her body, slamming into the lump that had formed in her throat. "No—" She shook her head. "No, I won't do that."

Logic told her he couldn't force her to leave his office without becoming physical. She didn't think he would do that in front of his receptionist. She prayed he wouldn't, but she flinched back instinctively as he raised his hand.

"Don't!" she cried.

"Don't *what*?" He ground out the question as he jerked loose his tie, letting it hang like a noose around his neck. "Is that what it takes to get rid of you? You need to be threatened, roughed up?"

"No!" Honor insisted. "Talk to me. Give me a chance."

"Mr. Starhawk," the receptionist broke in.

"Not now!" He waved the woman silent, his glare fixed relentlessly on Honor. "Get inside," he said, flicking his head toward his office door.

"You'll talk to me?" Honor was genuinely startled.

"I didn't say anything about talking, I said get inside."

She edged away from him, every sense alert. It had

never occurred to her that he might hurt her. Now she wasn't sure. His flying black hair and flared nostrils reminded her of the frightening legacy of his Apache heritage—*never forget, never forgive*. Even the expensive Italian-cut suit he wore did nothing to diminish the threat he exuded.

"You've got two choices," he said, moving toward her. "Get inside. Or get out."

He wanted her out, she knew that. He was trying to frighten her into bolting. And he was doing a damn good job. Despite the ultramodern surroundings, she couldn't shake the feeling that at any moment he might break through the thin veneer of civility and turn savage. Still, she couldn't back down. She would never be able to live with herself if she didn't follow through on what she'd started.

She turned and entered his office, listening for his footsteps behind her. Her throat went dry with fear as the door slammed shut. "I don't care what I've done to you," she said, whirling to face him. "I won't let you do this. I won't let you hurt me."

"Hurt you?" Something that might have been pain flared in his dark eyes. "I've never even touched you."

Honor fell silent, remembering vividly the one time they'd accidentally brushed up against each other— the shock, the incredible sexual pull. The chemistry between them had always been highly charged. Now it was explosive. "Why did you bring me in here then?" she asked.

He walked to his desk and shrugged out of his jacket, throwing it and his tie over the chair. The powder-blue shirt he wore created a strikingly beautiful contrast to his tawny skin. "Because I don't like to fight in public," he said, unbuttoning his cuffs.

"I didn't come in here to fight."

"That's unfortunate, because I did."

"But why?" she pleaded. "Why can't you let go of the past and deal with what's happening now? The tribe needs a high-profile attorney, Johnny. They need the best, and that's you. You're acting as if I destroyed your whole life, but it's not true. Look around you. Look at this office, it's beautiful. You have money, respect, a brilliant career."

He stopped rolling up his sleeves and glanced up at her, emitting a sound that was too harsh to be laughter. "There are lots of ways to destroy a person."

Again she caught the flicker of pain in his eyes. It held her, haunting her. She wanted badly to say something that would touch that pain, anything that would let him know she understood, but she sensed intuitively that sympathy would be dangerous. Only a fool tried to pet a wounded panther.

"We all get hurt," she said awkwardly. "Life isn't fair, but you have to move past the—"

"I did move past it, Honor. I was doing just fine until you showed up."

He'd cut her off so abruptly, she knew it was hopeless. There was no reaching him; he wouldn't allow it. Averting her eyes, she ran her hand down the sleeve of her silk blouse and cupped her elbow. When she looked up, he'd finished rolling up his sleeves and was opening a drawer in his desk.

He drew out an object that glinted in the light from the window. Honor couldn't see what it was, but fear struck at her heart as he came around the desk and started toward her. Caught in flashes of sunlight and shadows, he looked like some angry god of justice, a demon executioner sprung from hell.

She began to back up, not stopping until she hit a wall. "What is that thing? What are you going to do?"

"I want something to remember you by," he said.

"No, wait!" Her hands flew up, a gesture intended to protect herself more than to ward him off. A soft cry filled her throat as she realized what he had in his hand.

He raised a brass-lined sheath and thumbed a

lever that released a glistening knife blade. The snap and click it made, the slice of metal against metal, were nerve-shattering.

"No, Johnny—please!" Honor flattened herself against the wall, too horrified even to scream. The metallic *ching* of the knife reverberated in her brain. "What are you going to do?"

"Turn your head," he told her, his dark eyes flaring. He tipped the blade to signal the direction he meant.

Honor stared at him, frozen with disbelief. "Johnny, don't do this, you *can't.*"

"Don't delude yourself, Honor. You haven't even imagined what I'm capable of doing. Now turn your head," he said roughly.

She did as he told her, fear spilling into her mouth, scalding her throat with its vile taste. She waited for what seemed like several seconds of cold terror, and then she felt something heavy dragging on her hair. His hands? He was working at the coil she'd secured at her nape with an elastic band and hairpins.

There was a wrenching jerk against her neck muscles, and then, to her astonishment, her hair tumbled loose from its bonds, falling free around her face. A moan caught inside her as she realized what he'd done. And what it meant. He'd loved it when she wore her hair this way, loose and free. He'd told her that once. After he was sent away, she'd begun wearing it up, in the coil.

"Johnny, don't," she said, tears welling up as she turned to him.

He sheathed the knife and dropped it into his pocket.

"There," he said, stepping back to see what he'd done. A terrible, painful light suffused his eyes. "That's more like it. Now you're exactly the way I remember you—pale and golden, the angel of sympathy, sister-confessor to the poor, dumb Indian kid." A muscle worked in his jaw as he stared at her.

"Who would ever have guessed that the fair Honor Bartholomew was really a betraying little bitch? Not me. Sure as hell not me."

"Don't do this," Honor said, her voice choked with pain. "Please don't. I told you I was sorry."

"Don't give me *sorry*. Not now! Get out of my life. Give me some peace."

"I can't, Johnny." A sob racked her, and then another and another—aching, shuddering tremors that ripped her apart inside. "I have to do this. *Please* understand that. Let me find some way to make things right."

His head lifted, frozen in some kind of agony. Icy glints of pain and rage sparkled in the depths of his eyes. He shook his head slowly. "No, you can't make it right. You can only make it worse. Go—get out of here."

"Johnny, don't—"

He moved toward her, then checked himself. When he spoke, his voice was soft. "If you keep this up, Honor, I promise you I will hurt you."

Honor edged away from him. You're hurting me now, she thought. You're destroying me. Unable to say the words, she met his gaze and saw there a capacity for vengeance beyond anything she'd ever dreamed. Dear God, she thought, what have I done? Until that moment she hadn't truly understood how unforgivably she'd hurt him.

The boy he used to be flashed into her mind with his remote yet beautiful Apache pride, his shyness, and the traces of wonder in his dark eyes when he looked at her. *Johnny! What have I done?* Tears streaming down her face, she turned and left the room.

Honor didn't sleep that entire night. She sat in the wingback chair that was becoming her prison and wondered what was to become of her. There were no choices to be made this time, no question of flying home to safety. She was beyond that consideration. The past was a horrible, festering scar that had been reopened. She would either die of the rupture or find a way to heal it.

She would never have Johnny's forgiveness. He'd made that clear, but if she could bring him back to the reservation, even temporarily, if she could rebuild that one bridge, she would feel that she'd done something. Perhaps all she could do.

She was trembling from lack of sleep and a sick stomach when she entered Johnny's reception area the next morning. Given what she was facing, it was a miracle she wasn't in the throes of a full-blown panic attack. As it was, her nerves were raw, and she hadn't been able to keep down any food, not even a cup of coffee.

"He isn't here," the receptionist snapped, rising the moment she saw Honor.

"I think we've had this conversation before." Honor took a seat on the couch. "I'll wait."

"No you won't," the woman said, coming around her desk toward Honor. "Mr. Starhawk specifically said you weren't to wait. And he asked me to escort you out of the office if you showed up."

Honor sprang to her feet, trembling with the effort it took. "If you lay a hand on me," she said, "I'll slap you silly."

The receptionist stopped in her tracks, her eyes widening with surprise.

Honor was startled too. The threat had tumbled out before she could stop it. Queasy, she reclaimed her seat and whisked up an issue of *Town and Country*, leafing through the magazine determinedly to try to cover her shakiness. The lady she'd been raised to be abhorred confrontations, but if she couldn't win a minor skirmish with Johnny's secretary, she didn't stand a chance in the battle with him.

The receptionist returned to her desk and shot Honor an indignant but grudgingly respectful glare.

Honor felt a moment of mild triumph as she pretended to peruse the magazine. Having another human being regard her with anything other than glacial contempt was a welcome change after her encounters with Johnny. She'd come to think of herself as an emotional warrior in the last twenty-four hours, and as much as she needed to think in those terms to endure, her morale was desperately low.

As she continued to thumb through the magazine, the pictures and articles she'd only been half-aware of began to come into focus. The landscaped estates and lawn parties took her back to a happier time, before the tragic incident that split the Bartholomew family. They made her think of the woman of gentle breeding who'd reared her, Adele Bartholomew, her mother.

A bred-in-the bone New Englander from a fine old Vermont family, Adele would never have approved of Honor's behavior that morning. A lady didn't indulge in public displays of emotion, and she certainly didn't enter into arguments with "unpleasant people"—an elastic category that seemed to include anyone who didn't jump to do Adele's bidding, including officious secretaries. Now Honor realized how antiquated her mother's social codes had been, but she still loved and missed her terribly. Adele had been killed when Honor was only ten.

Honor, her twin brother, Hale, Jr., and their mother had been on their way to the airport for a family Thanksgiving in Vermont when a car ahead of them had a blowout and the Bartholomews' Rolls-Royce hit it head-on. The collision killed Adele and Hale, Jr., instantly. Honor sustained only minor injuries. It had seemed a miracle, but the emotional price she paid was enormous. In addition to the devastation of losing her loved ones, she'd had to deal with the guilt of being the only one who survived. Her father had stayed behind to conclude a business deal and was supposed to join the family that night.

Honor had never seen such naked pain in her father's eyes as when he learned his son was gone. Beyond the pursuit of power, the blond, tousled-haired boy had been the only thing Hale, Sr., had ever let himself love unrestrainedly. The blow had sent him into an emotional tailspin. Sadly he'd coped by burying himself in his work and avoiding his daughter. Eventually Honor realized it was because she reminded him so much of his son, and he had never been able to express his grief, but by then the damage to their relationship had been done. And the damage to Honor's self-esteem was almost as devastating. She felt unloved and deeply unworthy.

She'd entered her teen years an isolated child, largely unaware of her budding physical beauty. Miserable in boarding school, she'd begged her father to let her quit and attend a public high school. He'd agreed, but Honor hadn't been in any way prepared for the public school students' curiosity and, eventually, their animosity. Her unusual, quiet beauty and her father's wealth made her an outsider. She'd had no one to share her solitary dreams with, no one who cared enough to listen or try and understand . . . until Johnny.

Honor's hands were trembling as she closed the magazine on her lap. *No one but Johnny.* Yesterday in his office he'd called himself a poor, dumb Indian, but it was his intelligence that had first attracted her. She'd become aware of him on the high school's debating team. She'd watched his performances, seen how his fiery brilliance set him apart, and how the other students resented him for it. He'd worn his loneliness like a badge of courage.

After the trial he'd seemed to vanish from the face of the earth. She lost track of him completely until several years later, when she came across a news-

paper headline about three ex-marines who'd distinguished themselves in a daring mission to free
American prisoners in the Middle East. The media
had described the recovery work they'd been doing
for the Pentagon and dubbed them the "Stealth
Commandos."

Honor had been astonished to read Johnny's name
as one of the three men. He'd looked so different in
the photograph, she'd barely recognized him. His
hair had been cropped short, and he'd worn military
fatigues and aviator sunglasses. The photograph
had shown him with his two partners, Chase Beaudine and Geoff Dias. But it was Johnny who held her
attention. He'd looked rugged and hardened, as
though his military experience had been an exercise
in brute survival.

From that point on Honor had ferreted out every
bit of information she could find about the Stealth
Commandos. By the time the three men had retired
from recovery work, they'd been made national heroes
by the media. Johnny had gone into law and quickly
become the stuff of legend as the "courtroom warrior." Chase Beaudine, the man who'd formed the
group, had disappeared completely from the limelight, but Geoff Dias, "bad boy of the trio," according
to the press, had formed a mercenary-for-hire operation and remained very much in the public eye with
his daring exploits. . . .

Honor eventually became aware that she'd been
drifting in and out of the past all morning. Glancing
at her watch, she saw that it was early afternoon,
and there'd been no sign of Johnny. She felt weak
from fatigue and hunger, but she didn't dare nap or
leave to get food. She might miss him when he came
in.

As the afternoon wore on, the receptionist made
several hushed calls, rescheduling appointments.
Honor eavesdropped shamelessly but could hear
nothing except mumblings about a massage-therapy

session. She wondered if it was for Johnny or his receptionist. The woman could use some loosening up.

Eventually the receptionist began preparing to leave. "You going to stay the night?" she asked, giving Honor an exasperated look.

Honor tried to stand, but she couldn't get off the couch. Dizziness swamped her as she sank back down.

The receptionist rose, concerned. "Are you all right?" she asked.

"Just dizzy." Honor anchored herself to the arm of the couch and drew in a sustaining breath. "I'll be all right," she said, wondering if it was true as she looked up. "Apparently he isn't coming in today?"

"Even if he had come in," the woman said, seeming to take pity on Honor, "you wouldn't have seen him."

Honor glanced at his office door and realized immediately that he had another exit. Powerful men always had their escape hatches. Her father had his own private elevator that allowed him to get in and out of his office unobserved.

Suddenly Honor knew exactly where to find Johnny Starhawk. "Thank you," she said, managing to get to her feet. "Thank you very much."

Three

Honor's hunch proved true. She found Johnny's private elevator housed in a small room in the garage facility next to the fifteen-story building where Johnny worked. The two structures were linked by a sky-bridge, and the elevator required a key. Since Honor had no idea how to break into an elevator, she had little choice but to take up residence in that small room. It was just after 5:00 P.M., according to her watch, and she reasoned that if he had been in court all day, there was a chance he might stop by his office before going home.

The concrete rectangle wasn't built for comfort, but Honor settled herself on the floor in a corner and pulled the shirred skirt of her floral sundress down over her legs. She'd been so indoctrinated by her mother that girls wore skirts, not pants, that even now as an adult she gravitated toward dresses when choosing what to wear. She had pants in her ward-robe, including the jeans her mother abhorred, but skirts comforted her somehow. Perhaps they rein-forced a sense of family tradition that seemed to have been lost after Adele's death.

She rested her head against the wall and tried mentally to practice the things she had to say to

Johnny, but the fatigue that washed over her made it almost impossible to keep track of the points she wanted to make. Her thoughts slowed down like a record played at the wrong speed, warping into odd, disconnected fragments before they slipped away from her altogether. She hadn't eaten or slept in nearly twenty-four hours, and the combination of nerves, exhaustion, and hunger was taking its toll on her mental processes.

She closed her eyes, trying to concentrate, but with the darkness behind her lids came a strange lassitude, a heaviness so seductive she wanted to let go of everything and give in to it. She couldn't remember ever feeling so tired or weak. Within moments she was drifting in a state of semiconsciousness, floating somewhere between sleep and exhaustion, the heaviness dragging her down. She could feel herself sinking deeper and deeper, spiraling helplessly toward something disturbing. . . .

Terror seized her when she heard the hawk's scream. Its shadow swept the ground in front of her, causing her to whirl and look up. The sun was a fireball in the sky. It blinded her, and then its brilliance went dark, transformed into the soaring wings of a magnificent creature, a hawk with flashing eyes and flaying talons.

She screamed, begging for mercy as the creature swooped down on her. Its shadow engulfed her, and she was hit by a heaviness that knocked her to the ground. Her clothes were ripped away. Her arms and legs were pinned to the ground as the demon subdued her, overpowering her struggles. But before the creature could ravish her, it was transformed again, this time into a man. He was savage and terrifying, as magnificent as the hawk, his black hair flying like wings, his features covered with war paint.

And then she saw the knife. . . .

• • •

Honor screamed and screamed, one bloodcurdling shriek after another as a pair of hands closed on her arms and pulled her to her feet, anchoring her against the concrete wall.

"Honor! What happened? Are you all right?"

She struggled against her assailant, against the nightmare that wouldn't let go of her. The hawk's shriek was ringing in her ears. She could still see the warrior and the terrible flashing blade of his knife. At the same time, from somewhere outside of her, she could hear Johnny's voice. He was shouting at her, but it seemed a part of the dream.

"Honor, tell me what happened. Did someone hurt you? Were you attacked?"

She felt herself being shaken back to consciousness, and she opened her eyes. Haloed by the room's dim light, Johnny looked huge and terrifying. His grip on her arms was bruising, his eyes incandescent. "Let go!" she cried.

"I'm not going to hurt you," he said, trying to calm her. "What happened? For God's sake, Honor, tell me."

She twisted out of his arms, staggering backward. Overcome by dizziness and nausea, she slumped against the concrete wall and sagged to her knees.

"Honor!"

She shook her head, cringing as he knelt next to her. "It was terrible," she said. "He had a knife—"

"Oh, God," Johnny breathed. "Who had a knife?" He hovered near her protectively, as though wanting to help, but hesitant to touch her in any way. "Honor, who was it?" His voice rasped as he asked the next question. "Did he hurt you?"

"No—I don't know." A bewildered sob shook through her. "It was a dream, I think."

"A dream? You weren't attacked?"

"Yes . . . I was." When the shuddering finally

stopped, Honor gathered herself together and looked up at him. "By you," she said, knowing the terror she felt must have seeped into her eyes. "You had the knife."

She saw a flash of disbelief cross his face. His expression held regret and concern, as if he was struggling with an apology, but the words wouldn't come. Finally he stood up and took off his jacket, settling it over her shoulders. "Are you all right?" he asked. "Can you stand up now?"

"I think so." She drew up one leg and tried to stand, but she was shaking too badly to manage it.

"Come on, paleface . . . be strong."

Tears of astonishment sprang to Honor's eyes. He'd whispered the same thing years ago when he'd broken the news that he was being charged with assault. Looking up at him now, she almost thought she'd imagined hearing the words. They'd been low and harsh, but very gentle . . . *and he had spoken them*. She saw his outstretched hand, the long fingers, the rich brown skin. He was offering to help her.

Honor felt a stirring of disbelief as she put her hand in his. A sparkle of awareness ran up the inside of her arm, tingling her skin. He'd never touched her this way before, she realized. And perhaps she hadn't allowed herself to believe that he ever would. Tears welled up again, embarrassing her as she responded uncontrollably to the signals his touch communicated, the gentle strength, the warmth. Her defenses were down. She was overreacting to everything, especially to him, and yet she wanted to believe that some link might have been made between them, a tendril of friendship restored.

"I'm sorry," she said, clutching his hand. "It seems I'm always crying around you, always apologizing."

He didn't respond, but she felt his other arm brace her, supporting her until she was on her feet. They released hands slowly, their fingers brushing with tiny, awkward collisions, each exquisitely sensitive. Honor's breath shuddered as she released it. She had no protection. The sight of his burnished skin on hers, the feel of it, was a tripwire to her overwrought nerves.

"Thank you," she managed.

"It's okay," he said huskily. "My . . . pleasure."

Dizziness washed over her as she looked up at him. His pleasure? The thought of giving Johnny Starhawk pleasure of any kind brought her to a pitch of awareness that was almost painful. The shadings of emotion in his expression confused her. They were too complex to analyze, but she could see one thing clearly. Desire. It flickered like a candle flame in his smoky eyes.

Physical intimacy hadn't been a part of their teenage relationship, but there had always been an implicit sexuality. Even at fourteen, she'd been acutely aware of him as male, of herself as female. Perhaps it was the very force of their attraction that had kept them apart. One touch, one kiss, and they'd have been swept into something forbidden.

The thought of doing forbidden things with Johnny made her shudder inside. Dark images of entangled bodies flashed into her mind, animal images—the dangerous passion of the male panther, the excited cries of his mate.

"Are you all right?" he asked. "Do you need a doctor?"

She shook her head, grateful he'd brought her out of her strange fantasy. "I'll be fine once I get my bearings."

His jacket had fallen off her shoulder, and as he drew it back on, she noticed the marks on her upper arms. They were reddened and raised like welts. It took her a moment to understand what had happened. They'd come from Johnny's hands. His grip had been rough and urgent when he'd first pulled her to her feet. When she'd tried to get away, his fingers had cut into her arms. Hoping he wouldn't see the marks, she tugged the coat around her.

But Johnny had seen them. His eyes caught every tender red welt. Against her pale skin they looked like serious wounds, and the sight took him by storm. He was vaguely aware that she was pulling against him as he held the coat open, but he couldn't release his grip on the material. His gaze was riveted on the marks, and the feelings that hit him were beyond description. That he might actually have hurt her caused revulsion, but it was more than that. He felt a jolt of longing too. And need. Animal need. To touch the wounds, to heal them. *To claim the marks as his.* His heart was pounding with a force that almost suffocated him.

When he found his voice, it was a ragged whisper. "I always knew I'd leave marks if I touched you."

Honor went breathlessly still. He was beautiful and frightening, a man possessed. The traces of anguish in his voice mesmerized her. She tried to close the coat. She tried to remove his hand, but it was clenched around the linen material. The conflict in his eyes was horrible, but she couldn't let herself acknowledge it.

"I always wanted you to touch me, Johnny," she said. "I wouldn't care about marks, or anything else, if only you would touch me."

Johnny's hands locked, frozen between drawing her forward and holding her back. The turmoil inside him was agonizing. What was she doing? Offering herself? A lamb to the sacrificial altar? She couldn't possibly know how profound a temptation she was. He wanted her so badly, it felt like a destructive force, a rage that neither of them would survive if he ever released it. It astonished him that she didn't seem to fear what he might do to her. Didn't she understand that he couldn't even touch her without triggering that dark rage? That making love to her would be wildly dangerous?

He freed the coat and stepped back, his muscles aching from the sudden release of tension.

She looked up at him, bewildered. "It's all right. I'm not hurt." She seemed desperate to make him see that the marks didn't mean anything, that they weren't an omen of things to come. But Johnny was beyond reassurance. He was all tangled up inside, soulsick from wanting her and from knowing what he was capable of doing to her. He couldn't trust himself to get near her again. He would hurt her, one way or another, whether he wanted to or not.

"My decision is for the defendant in this case." The judge's sonorous voice boomed through the hushed courtroom. "In the matter of Beaumont Oil versus Ridgecrest Community Church, I find in favor of Ridgecrest Community Church."

The church's minister let out a gasp and flung his arms around Johnny. The man's wife broke down in sobs, and the crowd in the gallery came to their feet, cheering enthusiastically. It was a dizzy, exhilarating moment. Johnny clapped the minister on the back, then released him, a smile breaking on his face. The older man's joy was palpable, and as Johnny watched him turn to his weeping wife and embrace her, he felt a sense of great relief. Maybe he'd actually done something right for a change. If so, it was the first time in days.

"Hey, Starhawk! *Bonzai!*"

Over the heads of the hugging couple, Johnny's assistant flashed him a thumbs-up. The junior attorney was the very person Johnny wanted to talk to at that moment, but several members of the church's congregation rushed forward with congratulations, blocking the way.

Johnny took all the kudos in stride as he made his way over to his assistant and drew him aside. "You take it from here, Lone Ranger," he said under his breath, knowing he was giving the younger man a chance at the limelight. "Once you get our clients safely through this pack and outside, you can field the media's questions. Tell them this case has restored your faith in the American legal process. That's always good for a network sound bite."

"Where are you going?" his assistant asked with a surprised smile. "What about our victory party at Riley's Pub?"

"I need a break," Johnny said. "Relax and enjoy yourself. Your wickedly handsome mug is going to be splashed coast to coast on the five o'clock news. The barmaids over at Riley's will be panting for you when you get there."

After giving his assistant a few more last-minute instructions, Johnny slipped out a side door into the hallway. The press would be waiting out front, and if he moved quickly enough, he might escape without being noticed. There was one stop he had to make first, however. He fished in the pocket of his suit pants for his keys.

The men's room was empty when he opened the locked door and let himself in. A row of mirrors flashed his reflection back at him as he walked to one of the basins, and he was surprised at his resemblance to a civilized human being. Despite the excitement of winning a tough case, he half expected to see a wild-eyed beast snarling back at him. He hadn't felt civilized since the morning she'd walked back into his life. He'd barely felt human.

He turned on a tap and splashed cold water on his face, aware of the tension in his neck muscles. *Where was she?* he wondered. It was a question that had been on his mind all day. He hadn't seen her in over forty-eight hours, not since the incident at his private elevator. He should have been out celebrating her absence, but he couldn't help wondering if something had happened to her.

The water in his cupped hands felt icy and cleans-

ing as he brought it to his face, but there wasn't any
amount of water that could wash away the image of
her crumpled on the floor near his elevator. The terror
in her cries was seared into his memory cells. He'd
never thought of her as physically strong, and certainly not as the type of woman who could defend herself in a dangerous situation. She'd always seemed
vulnerable in that way, which was probably why he'd
felt compelled to massacre the arrogant bastards
who'd taunted her when they were kids. It had filled
him with guilt and fury that they were ridiculing her
because of her "redskin" boyfriend.

A whisper of cool air made him aware of the silk
material of his slacks against the back of his calves.
He raised his head, beads of water sluicing over the
angular bones of his face as he glanced in the mirror.
The double reflection he saw astonished him. The
one word he breathed was more than profane, it was
incredulous.

"What are you doing here?" he said, staring at
Honor's image in the mirror. He whirled, water flying, and raked a hand through his hair, tossing it out
of his face. "How did you get in here?"

The last thing he expected was the faint, trembling
smile she produced. She looked like a woman tilted
precariously on the brink of something risky, as if
she knew she was breaking the rules and had realized there was no point in taking half-measures. She
was also wearing the jacket he'd put over her shoulders the night he'd found her sprawled in front of his
elevator.

"This is yours," she said, touching the jacket's
lapel. "I thought I should return it."

"But how did you get in?"

A subtle vibrancy shimmered in the mists of her
blue eyes, like light rain on a sunny day. She was
pleased with herself, he could tell. "I caught the door
before it closed," she said. "I guess you didn't hear
me behind you."

"You do know this is a men's bathroom?" He half turned, pointing out basins, urinals, and stalls.

She took it all in, seemingly impressed. "If I didn't before, I certainly do now." Her smile wavered, and she wet her lips; but oddly, the nervous gesture made her seem more assured. "It's probably the only place in this building not overrun with people," she said. "By the way, congratulations on winning the case."

For the first time in a very long time, Johnny was dumbstruck. In his wildest dreams—and he'd had some wild ones—he'd never imagined America's favorite debutante following a man into the toilet. There was something different about her, he realized as he looked her up and down. It hit him like a blow to the rib cage when he realized what it was. She was wearing her hair down. It spilled around her shoulders, free and golden, just the way it had after he'd cut the coil with his knife.

She was dressed differently too. Besides his jacket, she wore blue jeans and a soft peach cardigan sweater that was unbuttoned at the neckline. The sweater's opening lay over the pale swell of her breasts, whispering hints of the shadowy crevice between them.

He doubted that it was intentional on her part, but God help him, she looked sexy—not nearly as sweet and demure as he remembered, or as contrite as he would have liked. He didn't need sexy, not from her. Not now! He had enough trouble where she was concerned.

"You called this meeting," he said abruptly. "I assume you've got something to say."

"Yes." The trembling smile reappeared. "You're wet."

Johnny touched the beads of water that clung to his jaw and swore softly. He pulled some paper towels from the dispenser and scrubbed the moisture away. "I wish I could say the same thing about you," he said, tossing off the double entendre without considering its impact.

The color fled her pale face, then crept back in a slow pink tide. But she said nothing, did nothing, as though shocked into some inner recognition of her own feelings, of his physical nearness, and of the fact that she was locked in a men's bathroom with him. Her mounting awareness was breathtaking to watch.

"If I were wet," she said, her voice barely audible, "that would be between me and my Calvins."

Johnny's breath went husky with male amusement. Something strange was definitely going on here. She was getting less predictable by the minute. He might have thought of a comeback if something else about her hadn't already captivated him. Violets. The scent of violets rose from her flushed skin like morning mists off a dewy meadow. He had an unexpected image of her standing naked and pale before him, wearing nothing but that lush scent. The vision left him fighting for breath. And fighting off memories.

The day he'd surprised her at her locker, he'd caught a whiff of the exotic, flowery scent she gave off. She'd been frightened and excited then too. Either her body chemistry enhanced her perfume, or she just naturally smelled of violets. He didn't know. He didn't care about anything except the havoc that fragrance had done to his mind and body.

He didn't want to remember the nights of sleepless yearning, dreaming about her violet-scented body underneath his, about her tender curves, and that first deep plunge into her virginity. He'd imagined the conquest in such pleasure-soaked, erotic detail that even now, all it took was a whiff of violets to make him harden and ache.

"What the hell are you doing here?" he asked. "I thought you'd taken flight, gone back to Arizona."

Honor was startled at his harshness. She didn't

have the quick answer he seemed to be demanding. She'd spent the last two days struggling with the repercussions of what had happened between them when he'd found her at the elevator. All he had done was touch her, but she'd been in a daze ever since.

That brief moment of kindness had reawakened her. His gentleness had revived needs and longings she'd wanted to believe were dead. But they were far from that; they were achingly alive. Her dreams, sleeping and waking, had been flooded with images of Johnny holding her, soothing all her fears away. She'd imagined tender touches and sweet kisses that would make her body burn with need.

This morning she'd come awake with a desire to see him that left her shaking. Just to see him, she told herself, that was all she needed . . . and maybe to be touched again.

"I came to finish what I started," she said. "With you."

He shook his head, as though weary of it all. "Dammit, I thought I'd frightened you off for sure."

"You told me to be strong."

"I didn't mean with me."

Honor met his searching gaze and forced herself to hold it. "Yes . . . you did." She'd spoken from intuition, without having any more than a subliminal understanding of what triggered her. But now that she'd committed herself, the premonition was so strong, she had to go on, even if it meant risking his anger. There were other things she knew about him.

"You're going to help the tribe, Johnny," she said, her voice softening as she realized that she was going to say what was in her mind no matter what he thought. "You need to be convinced, that's all. And I'm the one who's going to convince you, just as your grandfather predicted."

"My grandfather?"

"Yes." She rushed on, encouraged that he hadn't stopped her. "He's been having visions, prophetic dreams. He believes that you're the only one who can win their case in a court battle against Bartholomew Mines. His last dream told him who would bring you back."

"And it was you?"

She nodded. "What if he really does have the gift of prophecy, Johnny? If these things are foreordained, then aren't you wasting your time fighting the inevitable?"

Johnny's features darkened with frightening speed. "I don't buy my grandfather's mystical claptrap, and I never have. He predicted my birth would bring bad luck, and then two days after she'd delivered me, my mother killed herself. I think the old fool's predictions drove her to it."

Honor knew she had to proceed carefully. She was touching on the very origins of his alienation and pain. "But what if your grandfather simply foresaw that tragedy? And what if he's foreseeing something else now? A victory? It seems to me that he's offering you a way to come back, to replace the bad with something good. This could be a fresh start."

"Spare me the pep talk," he said coldly. "This is a package deal. If I buy into good omens, then I have to buy into bad ones. I have to believe in a crazy old man who made my life hell with his dreams and predictions."

"He was only following his beliefs, Johnny. Isn't it time to let go of the past? To forgive—"

She would have given anything to take back that last word, but it was too late. Johnny had turned away, his profile flashing along the room's mirrors in a strobelike effect that magnified his conflict. Honor was caught by his pagan beauty and his darkness. The rippling of so many images gave the illusion of revealing the inner man, of a mask stripped away, of naked glimpses of something desolate and beautiful inside him. It was rage, Honor realized, and sadness. The two elements were mixed together explosively.

She felt as if she'd been witness to some dark spot in his soul, as if she'd seen the bad omen.

He turned toward her, and something in his expression made her heart begin to throb. "What are you doing?" she asked as he started toward her.

"I want this back," he said.

She didn't know what he meant until he was standing before her, gathering up the lapels of the jacket she wore and drawing her toward him. Honor could feel his hands on her skin, the jutting bones of his wrists pressing against the softness of her breasts.

"Maybe I should take it off first?" she asked.

"I'll take it off." He drew the jacket off her shoulders, then let it drop to the floor behind her. The material slid down her back like heavy silk and pooled at her feet. At the same time she felt his hands close lightly on her shoulders.

"Oh, God," she said, breathing the words like a prayer.

She was riveted by his touch, a thrill of alarm rippling up and down her body. For a woman who'd had little experience with male sensuality, she was completely thrown by her own reactions. All he'd done was take off the coat, but the sensations he evoked were the most stimulating she'd ever known. As his thumbs nestled in the hollows beneath her collarbones, she emitted a soft sound of excitement.

Johnny felt himself dying inside as he took in her trembling anticipation. He'd given in to an irresistible impulse to take off the jacket and put his hands on her, never considering where it would go beyond that. Now how the hell could he stop at that? She was shaking, sighing. He was surging inside. But the impulse wasn't as hot and dark and volatile as the last time they were together, he realized. It was more sensual this time, less vengeful. *Could he make love to Honor Bartholomew without it turning into emotional warfare?*

The answer came hurtling back at him. No! Never!

But it was too late for nevers. He was already aroused, already in need of a woman.

"I wish to hell you'd go back to Arizona," he said, anger burning through him as he tilted her face up to his. "Look at us, dammit. Look what's going to happen if you don't."

"What?" she said, her voice throaty with fear, passion.

"This . . ." He bent toward her mouth, but the sound she made stopped him. It was sweetest thing he'd ever heard, soft and raspy, full of yearning. Her scent washed over him, drenching him in violets. Hothouse violets. Seductive violets. A blast of sexual longing shot through him, and his hands began to shake.

"Jesus," he breathed, releasing her so abruptly she staggered.

"What's wrong?" she asked.

Johnny caught his own splintered reflection in the row of mirrors. He looked like a wild man, one heartbeat away from doing something crazy. He wanted to make love to her all over the damn bathroom. He wanted to take her on the cold tile floor, and up against the wall. He wanted to set her on the basin and do it there too.

"I'm what's wrong," he said, sweeping back the dark hair that had fallen onto his face. He turned on her, quietly furious. "You could have anybody you want, your pick of nice guys. What do you want with me, a savage?"

"You call yourself that?"

"It has nothing to do with being an Apache. It's wanting things you can't have that makes you savage inside."

Her shoulders moved with a deep breath. "What are you saying? That you want me? Is that what you're saying?"

There was nothing Johnny could do to lock up the turbulence inside him. He couldn't deny the truth.

He'd wanted her when they were kids. He wanted her now, violently, and the only way he was going to keep from acting on his animal urges was to get her out of the room.

She smothered a gasp as his hand went to his zipper. "What are you doing?" she asked.

He flashed her a glance that was arrogant, potent, male. "This is a men's bathroom," he said. "I'm going to do what I came in here to do. Care to watch?"

He drew the metal pull tab down slowly, daring her not to notice that he was still aroused, hard as hell with desire. Her eyes widened with disbelief as he rode the zipper all the way to the bottom stop and reached inside to free himself.

"You're right!" she cried angrily. "You are a savage." She whirled and stalked toward the door, her blond hair flying.

As the door slammed shut behind her, Johnny was left to stand there, grimly aware of the empty, echoing room and of his own hand pressed against the hard throb at his groin.

Four

Honor ducked down behind the steering wheel of her rented Ford Escort as another luxury car rolled up to the high-rise condo across the street from where she was parked. It wasn't Johnny's crimson Ferrari Testarossa, but Honor watched anyway, curious about the other tenants in his building.

A flashy and fashionable young brunette alighted from the white Mercedes convertible and blithely turned her keys over to the valet-parking attendant. She gave the doorman a perky smile and a Miss America wave as she strolled up the red-carpeted promenade toward the monolithic glass doors. They slid open as if on command, though of course Honor knew the doorman must have entered an access code on the console at his station.

If she had a moment of concern about such a beautiful young woman living in Johnny's building, she was far more worried about dealing with the doorman when she made her own attempt to enter the building. Wondering if her plan was adequate, she glanced at the royal-blue tank top, drawstring workout pants, and tennis shoes she wore. The tote bag next to her on the seat was full of perfumed oils and towels.

Her *plan*? Panic rippled through her as she thought about the masquerade she was about to try to carry off. Skulking in parked cars and staking out luxury high rises wasn't at all her style. And crashing the guarded portals of one wasn't even in her realm of reality. The closest she'd ever come to anything regarding espionage was reading Nancy Drew mysteries as a child. She would never have considered such drastic measures if she hadn't been driven to it by the utter frustration of the last seventy-two hours.

Johnny had disappeared. He seemed to have dropped off the face of the earth. She'd been haunting his office, trying to pinpoint his whereabouts, ever since their encounter in the courthouse bathroom three days ago. She'd even hung out at his elevator for an entire day, but there'd been no sign of him.

His receptionist had turned into a sphinx whenever Honor was around, not speaking at all or in indiscernible whispers when she answered the phone. Honor's worst fear was that Johnny had left town, either on business or more likely just to avoid her, and she would never be able to find him. As that fear built, her determination to track him down had become an obsession.

She had to finish this dark and frightening game she'd started with him, no matter what happened, no matter what he did to her. She felt as if she'd blundered into a maze that merged past and present, and at every blind corner she was confronted with her own fears and desires. She wanted out, but something told her that Johnny was the key master. Only he knew the way.

The roar of a powerful engine gearing down alerted Honor. A gleaming red Testarossa had pulled up to the building. Honor sank down, her pulse quickening as the door of the idling sportscar flew open. Even her thinking processes were thrown off kilter as

Johnny swung his long legs out of the low-slung car and gracefully unfurled his dark length.

He rose to his full height, tall and catlike in the sun, his ebony hair lifting in the late afternoon breezes. The stone-washed jeans and white cotton T-shirt he wore caressed his rippling muscularity with the suppleness of an animal's coat. The scuffed cowboy boots added an unexpected rugged touch. Even dressed casually, he exuded the lean and hungry look that women found irresistible.

Just seeing him again made Honor's stomach flutter and clutch, as if she were an infatuated teenager. He didn't have to do anything, she realized. He only had to stand there and look gorgeous to stir up the sweet ache of her unfulfilled longings. Calming herself with a concerted effort of will, she watched as he walked toward the glass doors and disappeared inside the building. She would have to give him plenty of time to prepare, she reminded herself. It was crucial that he be ready when she got there, on the massage table and facedown. The last thing she wanted was to catch him in the act of undressing.

She glanced down at the tote bag full of exotic paraphernalia and released a taut breath. Panic welled up again, stronger this time. Whatever had possessed her to try such a thing? She had always been cautious and conservative by nature, raised to be unfailingly discreet and polite. She'd never been one of those reckless women who craved excitement and danger. The Bartholomews weren't thrill-seekers, nor did Honor want to be one. And yet here she was, preparing to go up to Johnny's suite and . . . A shudder extinguished the thought. If she let herself dwell on what she had to do, she would never make it out of the car. The idea of masquerading as a masseuse had come to her just yesterday when she'd been stationed in Johnny's office, hoping for some news of his whereabouts.

The receptionist had left for a break, notifying the

message service to take all calls. The phone rang several times before Honor was able to convince herself to pick it up. When she'd realized it was a massage therapist confirming Johnny's appointment for the next afternoon, Honor had acted on impulse. She'd pretended there was some mistake, double-checking with the woman to be sure she had the correct appointment time, then requesting the woman verify Johnny's home address. "I'm afraid Mr. Starhawk's out of town," she'd said, promising to re-schedule. When she'd hung up the phone, she'd laughed out loud.

But she wasn't laughing now. She would soon be bluffing her way past the doorman, into the building and onto an elevator that would take her up to Johnny's condo. The question that truly concerned her was how she would deal with Johnny if she actually got that far.

Moments later Honor stood in the sleek mirrored elevator, ascending swiftly and silently toward her fate. As the chrome door panels whooshed open, she stepped out into an anteroom that faced the double doors of Johnny's penthouse. She walked straight over and rang the bell, knowing any hesitation would be her undoing. To her profound relief, a maid answered.

"I'm from the International Health Spa," she said with brisk efficiency. "Mr. Starhawk has a four P.M. appointment. Sorry I'm a few minutes late."

The maid wasn't impressed. "Are you new?" she asked, scrutinizing Honor's features first, then her clothing. "You're not the one he usually uses, are you?"

Honor held her leather tote as though it were proof of her authenticity. "His regular massage therapist is ill today. I'm replacing her. Nearly fifteen years of experience." In a bookstore, Honor added silently. She was getting surprisingly good at subterfuge.

"This way," the woman said, leading Honor down a

long hallway hung with black-and-white photographs. Honor recognized an Annie Leibovitz print and a Paul Strand landscape, and reminded herself not to feel too sorry for Johnny. He had certainly prospered financially.

"He's in there," the maid said, pointing toward the last doorway on the left. "Go on in. He's ready for you." As the woman bustled away, she added over her shoulder, "I'll be leaving for the evening soon. You'll have to let yourself out when you're through."

"Thank you," Honor said, staring at the door the maid had pointed out. As she approached it and reached for the knob, she had the vague sense of a heartbeat pulsing in her fingertips. The pulse echoed in her ears, expanding until it seemed to be both inside and outside her body, resonating in the hallway itself.

"Go on in!" the maid called.

Honor started violently. Her fingers gripped the knob and turned it. The sound of the latch popping free created a small explosion in her brain. She gave the door a push and stood back as it swung open, revealing a panorama of spidery high-tech equipment. Not a sauna, she realized. Not even a bedroom as she'd feared. It was a personal workout room.

She stepped inside and shut the door behind her, aware of the low and soothing strains of classical music. The man stretched out on the massage table across the room from her appeared to be sleeping, his hands folded under his head, his face turned away from her. She knew it was Johnny by the bronze skin and the long hair spilling into the curve of his far shoulder. But other than that, there were no familiar markers. He was naked, she realized. Only a narrow white towel covered his buttocks.

Dear God. Naked.

Honor brushed a tendril of hair off her face, forcing it back into the ponytail she wore. Smothering a gasp, she dropped her tote and quickly wrestled free the elastic band that restrained her hair, wincing as she yanked out several strands. The last time she'd worn her hair back, it had provoked him into pulling a knife on her. She didn't want to risk that reaction again!

Once she had her hair free, she approached cautiously, negotiating a bewildering array of equipment. She rubbed her hands together in an attempt to warm them, her gaze drawn to the coppery muscles that rippled down the length of his back. They sloped with the curve of his spine and rose powerfully to that most potent of areas on the male body, the part of him that was covered with the towel.

Honor had never gone in for male calendar art, but she couldn't imagine any paid model striking a pose half as erotic as the way Johnny was stretched out before her. His muscles were beautifully elongated, sinuously stretching the length of his entire body. Masculine power flowed like ocean currents under his dusky skin, a latent force.

She clasped her hands in a prayerlike gesture. Maybe he would sleep through the whole thing and never realize she'd been there. Better yet, maybe she could simply wait for twenty minutes and leave without even touching him. If he was asleep, who would know the difference?

He stirred as if drifting out of a catnap. "Any time you're ready," he said, his voice muzzled by his folded arms.

Honor's heart nearly dropped to her feet. So much for not touching him!

"There's some tension in my neck and shoulders," he mumbled, sounding drowsy. "Maybe you can work it out."

"Your neck?" She tried for a husky tone, hoping he wouldn't recognize her voice. The vial of oil she pulled from her tote was scented with orange blossoms, and the fragrance seemed to explode with tangy richness as she poured a few drops into her palm and rubbed her hands together, lightly coating them.

Her hands wouldn't stop trembling as she antici- pated the incredible intimacy of touching him. Why had she thought she could do this? At what point had she abandoned her common sense and lost contact with reality? She hadn't actually planned to go through with the massage. It was simply a way to get into his condo, to get past all the physical and psychological barriers that his office and the court- room presented. She'd thought they might be able to talk like two normal people if they were in his personal space, without the formality of business suits, teakwood desks, and watchdog receptionists.

Obviously she'd been so caught up in her plans for crashing the gate, she hadn't considered the pitfalls of trying to have a normal conversation with a naked man. Under the circumstances even a momentary massage seemed dangerous, yet she couldn't help wondering what he would feel like. His muscles looked as hard as steel, and yet they moved so fluidly, she was sure they must be supple to the touch.

It wouldn't have to be intimate, she told herself. A body was a body. She could pretend this one be- longed to someone else. Some man. Any man. But even she, who was masquerading as a masseuse, couldn't manage such a wild leap of the imagination. It was Johnny she was about to touch. Johnny, in all his stormy native beauty. The boy who'd loved her. The man who hated her . . .

She closed her eyes and took a calming breath, laying her hands on him. Several seconds flashed by before she could do anything more than rotate her palms. He *was* steel. But he was supple too. His muscles were dense, vibrant, alive. His body was cooler than she'd expected, and yet there was a flow of heat beneath the skin that seemed to respond to her touch. Every cell in her palms was alert, as if hungry for the feel of him. Finally, bravely, she splayed her hands over the breadth of his shoulders, aware of the unsteadiness in her fingertips as she worked them into corded muscle and sinew.

"Is something wrong?" he asked, shifting as if to look up.

Her eyes flew open, and she applied more pressure, ready to hold him down if necessary. "It's your arms," she said, making her voice husky to disguise it. "Why don't you put them down at your sides."

He unfolded his arms and did as she asked. Still looking away from her, he rested his head on the mat, giving her a clear view of his profile. It was impossible to avoid noting the sensual curve of his lips or the way his eyelashes lay against the arc of his cheekbones, almost lush in their length and thickness.

Relaxation brought out the natural sensuality in his features, she realized. But other than his eyelashes, there was nothing soft in his profile. A woman would have to be blind not to notice the arrogant cords that rode his neck and the vein ridging his high forehead. The capacity for retribution lay in his very bones; even his jawline was shadowed with it. He looked quite capable of torturing a woman half to death . . . but not with pain, with pleasure.

Her pulse rate surged, sending blood into her extremities, heating her thoughts and her actions as she worked at the tautness in his neck and shoulders. As his muscles began to melt under her efforts, his skin glowed warm and alive.

"That's good," he said. "You're good. Have I had you before?"

Honor sucked in a sharp breath and forced herself to keep up the pace and the pressure of her movements. A faint film of perspiration broke out on her upper lip. "No, you haven't . . . had me before."

"That can be remedied," he said, his voice low,

husky with male interest. "I want you on a regular basis."

"I'll see what I can do." Honor's imagination caught fire. What was he talking about? Did he mean doing something beyond a therapeutic massage? Did he mean having sex? Was that what he did with the women who came up here? The thought of him with another woman was like a match striking against her raw nerves. The image burst into quick, hot flames, horrifying her, but it was also disturbingly riveting in some way she didn't understand at all.

It was easy to imagine Johnny having sex. He was a beautiful, virile animal. He could put a woman in heat just by looking at her. What she couldn't imagine was his wanting a woman for anything more than that. Not for love. Never for love. A question flared painfully in her mind. Had she ruined him for that? For loving a woman?

As she stared down at her own hands, pale against his sienna-colored skin, she remembered the moment he'd offered his hand to her. *Come on, paleface, be strong.* She could still hear the emotion resonating in his voice as he said those words. And his passion in that dingy men's bathroom. He'd been shaking with it. What if he'd given in to the passion? she wondered. What if he'd taken her right there in that locked room? Would it have been love? Or sex?

A nerve near her mouth tautened, triggering a deeper, sharper contraction in her stomach. What if he had . . . taken her there in that room? She could still feel his hands on her arms, lifting her to him. She could feel his breath hot on her lips as he bent to kiss her. Taking a deep breath, she let herself imagine that kiss in all its fiery anguish. . . .

Her head tilted back deeply as his mouth came down on hers. The burning sweetness of his lips caught her soul on fire. It brought a whimper of helpless need to her throat. She wanted more of him. She wanted his teeth and his tongue and his hands. She wanted to be eaten alive by the panther, devoured by his passion. In her mind she could see his hard, hungry body pressing down on top of her, pressing into the tender ache between her legs. . . .

A low groan of pleasure brought Honor out of her fantasy.

It was Johnny who'd made the sound, she realized, and it wasn't difficult to see why. She was massaging his body with incredibly sensual strokes, her fingers undulating like waves, the balls of her palms rotating deeply, wantonly, into his lower back. In a burst of delayed awareness she saw that the heels of her hands were kneading his flanks and—

Sweet heaven! The towel had slipped off his body and fallen to the floor! A choked sound filled her throat.

Johnny's senses registered the distress signal, but only partially. It came to him from the depths of a warm, slumberous state. He shifted, becoming aware of pleasant sensations stirring inside him, of a tingling fullness in his groin. The towel seemed to be slipping and sliding over his backside, and he thought for a moment that she was removing it. Or was she replacing it? Either way she was a woman who got behind her work.

"Everything okay down there?" he asked.

She fumbled, then tucked the towel under his hips on both sides, making him up as if he were a bed. "Now it is," she said, her voice strange and breathy.

He smiled, wishing he could get a look at her. "My legs could use a little work when you get around to it, especially the inside of my right thigh. I pulled a muscle playing racquetball."

She made a funny choked sound again, and this time it got his full attention. What was she doing? He'd said thighs, but she was down around his ankles. And her hands were shaking noticeably. The scent of orange blossoms was rich and overpowering as he lay there, pondering her strange attraction to his feet. There was something about her voice too. He couldn't pinpoint it exactly, but . . .

"Ahh, that's good," he murmured as her hands crept up his right calf. He closed his eyes, relaxing, breathing deeply of orange blossoms. The fragrance was strong, but he kept catching whiffs of another perfume underneath it, something subtler and flowery. He inhaled several more times before he finally was able to put a name to it.

"Violets?" he said under his breath.

"What?"

"Nothing." Johnny grew very still, aware of every dip of her thumbs, every swirl of her fingers. His brain began to calculate ever so slowly. So what if he'd heard a vaguely familiar voice and smelled some violets. It didn't mean—

Oh, no . . . *oh, God.* Was that Honor massaging him? Were those her hands on his body? He ceased breathing for a second as a shock wave of awareness rolled over him. The circular motion of her fingers was magnified a thousand times in his mind, every delicate touch, every trembling caress. The heat that came off her palms seeped into his veins, firing his bloodstream.

It *was* her! Honor.

He felt a wild surge of excitement, an aching jolt of need, in his groin, and then reality came hurtling at him like a brick heaved through a window. It slammed into his chest with such force he couldn't breathe. What the hell kind of trick was she pulling now? What was she trying to do to him? Torture him? He'd done everything short of having her arrested, but she wouldn't back off. Apparently Miss Manners was willing to do anything to get what she wanted, including violating his personal privacy and driving him crazy with lust.

Anger began to smolder and burn, kindling his male pride, his Apache pride. He'd been sandbagged a time or two in his life, but this woman was the champ. She'd been playing Tiddly Winks on his backside and getting her jollies for twenty minutes now while he moaned and purred like a mangy tomcat. She'd even got him hard, the little witch!

"My leg," he said, clenching his jaw against the angry impulses that surged through him.

"What?"

"The right thigh, inside. Work it out." He opened his legs and heard her gasp.

"You want me to—"

"Do it, dammit!"

She sounded as if she were struggling for air. And then her fingers began to creep upward, stealing into the V of his thighs and driving him wild with their fluttering lightness. He clenched his jaw against the sweet riot of stimulation. When she touched the pulled muscles, he groaned aloud.

"I'm sorry!" she cried.

He caught hold of the towel and whirled up to a sitting position, snagging her by the wrist. "Sorry?" he said, pulling her toward him. "You haven't even begun to be sorry."

Honor was paralyzed by the surprise attack. Raw panic shot through her. She tried to twist away, but he caught her arm and whipped her back around, subduing her easily. His strength was astonishing. She quieted with a shudder, knowing it was futile to fight, perhaps even dangerous.

"What are you doing here?" he asked. "Why are you doing this to me?"

"It was a mistake, I—"

"No, this was no mistake. You don't have any more mistakes coming. You're over your limit."

His eyes were so black, she looked away. "Please," she implored softly. "I wasn't thinking straight. If you let me go, I'll—"

He imprisoned both her wrists in one hand and brought her chin up, forcing her to look at him. "What in the hell's wrong with you, coming up here?

Don't you know what I could do to you? Don't you know what I *want* to do to you?"

She started to shake, and within seconds the quaking of her body was so pronounced, she could hardly speak. "Yes . . . I know."

But she didn't know. She thought he was talking about sex, and he was, of course. He wanted like hell to be inside her, to violate her golden body with his hard, dark sex. He wanted to take her every way a man could take a woman—a virgin schoolgirl, a blushing bride, a whimpering female animal. He wanted that so badly it hurt. But sex wasn't enough. Sex wouldn't heal him. Only justice could do that, biblical justice. An eye for an eye. Her tears for his.

A skein of her hair was trapped between his hand and her flushed cheek. As he released the white-gold strands, he realized she was wearing her hair loose and free. "Is this for me?" he asked.

"No! I was afraid you would— I didn't want you to—"

"To what?"

"To go crazy, pull a weapon again."

He almost laughed. "Which weapon are we talking about? The knife? I wish I had one handy."

"Why? Why do you want to frighten me?"

He pulled her close, pleased at the tremulous sound she made. "Because I have to do something to you, Honor. I have to do *something*, for God's sake. And frightening you seems the safest choice."

Angry tears sparkled in her eyes. "Well, you've done it, all right? I'm terrified. Now can I go?"

He hesitated, considering that possibility, wishing he could let her go. How easy everything would be if she simply walked out and never came back. But it wouldn't work, and they both knew it. This wasn't over yet. She wasn't frightened enough. She'd be back.

"Go?" he said, lowering his voice. "Just when things were getting hot?" He released the towel, letting it fall to the floor, and then he brought her clenched hand to his thigh. She tried to draw back, but he tightened his grip, intending to force her into a direct confrontation with the evidence of how thoroughly she'd aroused him. He wanted her to know he was naked and hard. He wanted her to know the games were over.

"No, please," she pleaded.

"See what you do to me," he said, his voice as hard and pained as his body. "See how hot things are." He wanted her to look at him, to face the reality of her crazy scheme. When she wouldn't, he brought her hand to the wedge of dark hair. "You've tortured me enough for one lifetime. It's time I returned the favor."

Color spiked in her pale cheeks, two vibrant slashes of scarlet staining her porcelain skin. Johnny's hand tightened on her wrist as she stared up at him. Her eyes flashed with frustration, fire rising out of the mists. But it wasn't the defiance shimmering in her gaze that struck him; it wasn't even the excitement. It was guilt and contrition. Beneath the frustration she was searching his face with the sweet agony of a penitent.

"Johnny, please," she whispered. "I didn't mean to hurt you, I wasn't trying to—" Her voice broke.

Tears glittered in her eyes as she unfurled her fingers and touched him, cool silk against the molten core of his desire.

The softness of her hands sent him into a rage of need. He gripped her by the arms and brought her to his mouth, hissing out his pent-up fury, whispering of her betrayal, shuddering with naked longing as their lips touched. He wanted her. Sweet God, how he wanted her. And how he hated her for making him want anything.

The force of his own needs hit him. His breath rushed, mingling with hers. The quick, hungry touch of their lips, the little sounds she made, were exquisite. But some vital part of him made him hold back.

He couldn't allow himself the wild satisfaction of pulling her beneath him and driving into her.

She swallowed a sob, bringing him the most perverse kind of pleasure imaginable. She tasted like heaven, like everything he'd ever wanted and been denied. Yearning swept him, the awful, uncontrollable yearnings of childhood. As she pressed against his naked body, he pulled her into his arms, kissing her hungrily, unaware until that very moment that he was a starving man, a dying man. . . .

"Johnny?" she whispered, searching his features.

He was barely aware that they'd stopped kissing, that she was looking at him with the same kind of hope, the same frightened innocence, of the girl who'd betrayed him.

"What are we doing, Johnny?" She touched his mouth with shaking fingers. "What's happening between us? Is this love? Or sex?"

Love? Sex? The question seemed vital to her, but he didn't know what she was talking about. He needed her, he had to be inside her. His groin throbbed painfully with that need. But another feeling burned into his awareness as she continued to hold him back, caressing his mouth.

"What do you want it to be?" he asked.

She couldn't speak, but her eyes told him what she wanted. Her sweet sinner's eyes. She wanted love and forgiveness, absolution for her guilt, no matter what it cost him to give it. That was what was driving her, he realized. Not some selfless need to help his tribe, or to ease Johnny Starhawk's suffering. She didn't give a damn about the hell she was putting him through, the anguish. She wanted redemption, and he was the only one who could give it to her.

He caught her by the wrist, holding her seductive fingers away from his mouth. What *was* happening between them? Was he playing into her hands again? Literally, this time? As he stared at her imploring gray eyes, he realized her vulnerability was the most powerful manipulation he'd ever encountered. She'd destroyed him today with her whimpers of need and her fluttering fingers. She'd turned him inside out. Worse, she'd had him on the run since the day she'd arrived. She'd haunted his office, broken into a men's bathroom, and lied her way into his apartment. She'd been calling all the shots, running the show. But no more. That was all about to change.

"What's happening between us isn't sex," he said. "And it sure as hell isn't love. It's a felony called breaking and entering. And you just committed it."

"A felony?" she said, trying to cling to him as he released her and pushed her out of his way.

He sprang from the table, picked up the towel, and tied it around his hips as he strode across the room. An intercom unit was built into the opposite wall, and he jabbed a sequence of buttons. "Security," he said. "I've got an intruder in my apartment. Come up and get her, would you?"

He turned to look at Honor's ashen features, wishing to God he could bring her the same kind of turmoil she brought him. Just once. "If she gives you any trouble," he told the security guard, "call the police."

Five

Honor sat on the unmade bed of her hotel room, absently leafing through the pages of the morning newspaper, aware of the television cable news station droning in the background. She wanted distractions that morning, anything that would take up time and fill the silence until the bellman came to pick up her bags.

The heaviness that came with resignation had settled in on her since her encounter with Johnny the day before. A nagging sense of defeat still dragged at her breathing, and yet she was relieved to be going home. No one could say she hadn't given it her best shot. She'd done everything but physically kidnap Johnny to get him back to Arizona.

The shaman was wrong, she realized. She wasn't the one destined to bring Johnny back. Their past had been so much in the way, she hadn't even been able to make him see how important it was that he return to the reservation. That was what saddened her the most now. Her own sense of guilt was insignificant compared to what the White Mountain tribe would suffer if it didn't have adequate legal counsel.

She closed the paper at the same time that a news

flash came on the television. Glancing up at the screen, she saw an Indian boy being taken into custody by two sheriff's deputies.

"Problems on an Arizona Indian reservation," the commentator said. "A sixteen-year-old Apache boy is alleged to have dynamited the leaching operations at the Bartholomew uranium mines in the mountains near Coyote Gulch, Arizona. A spokesman for the Apache tribe claims toxic seepage from the mine's holding pools is polluting their pastureland water and contaminating their livestock. But the district attorney says he will show no leniency in this controversial case. The boy will be prosecuted to the fullest extent of the law."

Honor rushed to the TV and turned up the volume. She was shocked to see her own father appear on the screen standing next to the district attorney. Hale Bartholomew had grown thinner and craggier in the decade since she'd seen him, but with his steel-gray hair and piercing blue eyes, he looked no less intimidating.

Conflict rose inside Honor. She still loved her father and probably always would, no matter what he'd done. In some strange way she'd felt responsible for his happiness after Hale, Jr., and her mother died. She had longed to make up for the terrible loss he suffered, and perhaps she had hoped he would come to love her the way he had his son. Undoubtedly that was one of the reasons she'd let him talk her into testifying. Even now she didn't question that her father believed he was doing the right thing by having Johnny sent away. He'd thought he was "protecting" her. She wondered if he was any more capable today than he had been then of understanding that his need to play God and to manipulate other people's lives was cruel and self-serving.

"Outlaw behavior cannot be tolerated," Hale was saying. "If we don't make an example of the boy, we're encouraging other young renegades to take the law into their own hands."

Young renegades. He'd used that same phrase eighteen years ago. After the trial she'd overheard him congratulating the prosecutor, telling him his victory had sent a valuable message to any other "young renegades" who thought they were exempt from the American system of justice. That was when Honor first began to realize she'd made a terrible mistake.

She hit the TV's Off button and plunged the screen into blackness. The hotel room with its unmade bed, closed curtains, and soiled water glasses looked dingy and sordid as she surveyed it. Despair welled. She walked to the bed, intending to throw the newspaper in the trash, but a front-page article caught her eye as she picked up the paper. She scanned the piece hurriedly, realizing it was the same story she'd just heard on television, only it elaborated on the tribe's futile legal struggles and quoted a tribal spokesperson, who described the boy's act as a "cry of despair and frustration against an unresponsive system."

"Ma'am?"

Honor started, nearly dropping the paper. A bellman hovered in the doorway of her room.

"Are you ready to go?" he asked.

She nodded, but as he began to load her baggage onto his cart, she realized she couldn't leave Washington, D.C., not just yet. "Take the bags down and put them in storage for me, would you, please?" she asked, fishing some bills out of her purse and dropping them on the bed when she saw that his hands were full. "And thank you!"

Newspaper firmly in hand, she rushed past him and out the door.

• • •

Johnny was slipping on his double-breasted suit jacket to go out to lunch when his office door burst open.

"**Don't even think** about telling me to leave," said Honor, entering the room and shutting the door behind her. "And don't try calling security. I'm in no mood to be bullied this morning, Mr. Starhawk."

She remained by the door, a newspaper clutched in her hand. She was obviously frightened, but just as obviously determined to tough it out, whatever "it" was. Her eyes glittered with a determination he'd never seen before, and the effect was oddly exhilarating. Her blond hair was tied back, defying him to try to free it. Go ahead, her huge gray eyes seemed to be saying, pull a weapon on me. I'll show you just how savage *I* can be.

Good, he thought, his pulse quickening. She's good. If the anger vibrating in her voice was any indication, there would be no more tearful apologies, skulking around elevators, or sneaking into condos. She'd been pushed to the wall, and she was fighting back.

"Your scalp is safe," he said nonchalantly. "All my knives are out being sharpened."

She blinked. "I'm surprised you don't keep a spare hatchet or two."

He let out laughter, a husky, appreciative sound. So Honor Bartholomew had a dark side. God, he loved it. Normally he wouldn't have done anything to encourage her, but the glint in her eyes was too provocative to ignore. He let his gaze flicker disrespectfully over her pink mouth and linger at the neckline of her blouse. Her breasts shivered softly, deliciously, with each breath she took. What color were her nipples? he wondered, unable to check the irreverent thought. Pale pink, like her lips? Were they aroused? Was she aroused at the mere sight of him, the way he was at the sight of her?

"I'm not here for *that*," she informed him hotly.

"It doesn't matter what you're here for," he said, wishing he could make her understand what she did to him, what happened when she got within ten feet of him. "Just seeing you is enough, Honor. That's all it takes to get me going. I'm like one of those pacing animals at the zoo, agitated by the spectators, crazy to get at them."

"Why do you make it sound as if I'm purposely taunting you?"

"Aren't you? You make me want what I can't have, and that's the definition of savage, remember?"

She looked startled, but her surprise quickly changed to something else. Anger? A deep flush of sensual awareness crept up her throat. "That's not true. You could have had anything you wanted, Johnny. You wouldn't let yourself."

He was silent a moment, catching his breath. She was so honest it hurt. He could have had her, it was true. He could have her now, on the desk, on the floor, wherever they landed when he pulled her into his arms. She might resist, but that wouldn't last past the first kiss, and they both knew it.

"You're right," he said softly. "Nobody's stopping me. Nobody but me."

There was a catch of wounded pride in her voice when she finally spoke. "You've made it clear you don't want anything to do with me."

"Oh, *please*, woman, don't get coy on me! Not after all that painful honesty. I want to do everything there is with you. I'd like to violate you within an inch of your sweet life. Right now. Right here! But where you're concerned, I am that animal in a cage. And when that cage door comes open, somebody's going to get hurt."

She wet her lips nervously, and he told himself that he'd done all he could. He'd warned her what could happen, what he knew *would* happen if they ever made love. There was too much rage mixed up in his desire for her.

She held up the newspaper, almost defiantly. "Despite what you may think, I didn't come here to talk about sex and animals. I'd like you to take a look at this."

"What is it?"

Without a word she approached his desk and practically threw the paper at him.

"My goodness, have we forgotten our manners?"

"Read it," she snapped. "*Please.*"

He glanced at the headline and sighed heavily, dropping the paper to his desk. "The White Mountain thing again?"

"Read it!" she insisted. "Look what's happened."

"Honor, I don't care what's happened. It's not my fight."

"There's a sixteen-year-old boy involved," she said, overriding his resistance. "He's blown up my father's leaching plant, and they're going to crucify him, Johnny. He'll be a scapegoat."

Johnny glanced down at the paper involuntarily. Anger rose inside him as he skimmed the first two paragraphs of the article. Old anger. Brand-new hot anger. She was resurrecting his past and shoving it in his face! "You do know how to set a trap, don't you?" he said, glaring up at her.

"It happened, Johnny. I didn't make it happen. I'm just telling you about it. Can't you do something?"

"Like what?"

"Like defend the boy! Keep him out of jail or something equally damaging. Surely you don't want him to suffer the way you did."

"He won't." A nerve sparked in his jaw, jabbing at him like a hot wire. His anger sharpened and darkened with the need to hurt her back. "If I suffered, it was because of you."

She flinched, then caught herself. "Apparently you intend to punish me forever for a mistake in judgment that I made at fourteen." She threw up her hands in despair. "If I can't make you see how self-defeating that is, then at least understand that you're the one who's making the mistake now, a terrible mistake. You're not hurting me by refusing to help the tribe, you're hurting them."

"I owe them nothing."

"That isn't true. You owe them something simply because you have Apache blood running in your veins. You lived on that reservation. You know the truth. They're an oppressed people, struggling to defend their land against exploitation, just as they always have. Except now they're trying to do it legally, and they're at a terrible disadvantage. You have the skills to help them. Dammit, Johnny–"

She broke off in frustration, her gray eyes sparkling as she fought tears.

He stared at her, feeling his stomach muscles knot up but refusing to let the pain she evoked control him this time. "They have access to attorneys," he said.

"Right, and my father has money and influence. Hale Bartholomew doesn't need justice on his side. He can buy it! You should know that better than anyone." She pointed toward herself emphatically. "I'm not trying to excuse anything I've done, but surely you know that I didn't testify against you because it was something I wanted to do. My father put pressure on me. He misled me and misconstrued things—"

"Your father's a bastard," Johnny said, cutting her off coldly. "You don't have to convince me of that. But he wasn't my friend, Honor. You were. My only friend."

She shook her head and sighed out a sound full of regret, full of heartache and despair. "This could be your chance," she said at last, all the hope draining out of her voice. "If any of that hatred in your heart is directed at my father, then you're being handed an opportunity to avenge yourself. If you won't do it to help the tribe, then do it to stop Hale Bartholomew."

Johnny began to button the gray silk suit jacket, his fingers rigid. "I was just going to lunch."

Her mouth formed tight white lines at the corners, and she stepped back from his desk. "Apparently I've kept you. Another unforgivable sin." She turned and walked to the door, fumbling with the knob as she tried to let herself out of his office. "Enjoy your meal," she said, and left.

Johnny released his coat, letting it drop open. His gaze fell away from the closed door, but he remained where he stood, unmoving, until the hollow sensation in his chest made him draw in a breath. She wouldn't be back, he realized. He'd finally driven her off. Whatever he'd expected to feel at this moment, it wasn't this terrible emptiness. He had no sense of victory, not even of relief, except in the fact that an emotional train wreck had narrowly been avoided.

He wanted to tell himself that it was better this way, but the cliché stuck in his throat. It would have been better if they'd never met. Or if she'd never befriended him . . . but he didn't want to think about that now. The anger was gone, and for the moment, he felt nothing. He was one of nature's voids, waiting to be filled.

Staring at the door, remembering her fear and defiance, he recognized a stirring of something that was wholly unfamiliar to him where she was concerned. Finally, reluctantly, he gave it a name— admiration. She had guts and tenacity. She was either a stronger woman than he'd given her credit for or a very foolish one. If their roles had been reversed, he would have given up long ago. But then he knew what a nasty S.O.B. Johnny Starhawk could be. She only thought she knew.

He glanced down at the newspaper on his desk, pulled it to him, and began to read.

• • •

Honor switched off the air conditioner and rolled down the window of her Dodge Shadow, letting cool mountain air bathe her damp neck and forehead. The White Mountain Reservation with its scenic vistas and abundance of rivers and lakes was a refreshing change from the arid flatlands she'd been traveling through for the last several hours. White-river, the mountain town where the tribal headquarters was located, might have been any other small southwestern town, except that it was bordered by a serene river and its inhabitants were Apaches.

Honor turned onto a road shaded by cottonwoods that led to the tribal headquarters where she was to meet Chy Starhawk and other members of the tribe. The medicine man had been vague about who would be there, in the same way that he was enigmatic about almost everything, but Honor's primary concern was the bad news she was bringing him.

She pulled up in front of the log cabin–type building and let herself out of the car, surprised as she looked up to find Chy Starhawk standing before her in fringed buckskins, a beaded choker necklace, and a red cloth headband. Ceremonial eagle feathers floated from the tied ends of his headband, making him a splendid sight. He seemed to have materialized out of the tribe's proud but war-ravaged past.

Honor wondered whether he'd just performed a ritual of some kind, or whether the traditional clothing was for her benefit. She decided not to ask. It seemed an intrusion. From what she knew of the culture, Apaches were inclined to be private about their tribal traditions, especially sacred ceremonies.

"Johnny isn't coming," she told the old man as they entered the headquarters. "I'm terribly sorry."

The shaman neither stopped nor showed any emotion. "If you are sorry about things you can't change," he said, "you will soon not know the difference."

Honor almost thought she'd understood him. There wasn't time to mull meanings, however, because Chy had several people for her to meet. He introduced her to the tribal leader, a tall man in his late forties who wore jeans, cowboy boots, and a white Stetson over his long black braided hair. Johnny's godmother, the woman who'd advised her not to try to find Johnny after the trial, was heavier and grayer, but with the same unchanging quality of beauty in her rounded features. Other members of the council were present, as was the lawyer from the Indian Legal Services, a young man who was part Apache and part Zuni.

Honor hadn't expected such a prestigious group, and it made her aware of how vital her mission had been to them. This was more than a whim of Johnny's grandfather, she realized. Either the tribal leaders had believed his prophetic dream, or they'd reached the point of desperation and saw her as their last resort.

Either way it was that much more difficult to tell them she'd failed. Only the shaman showed no disappointment or emotion. Honor tried to be encouraging. She begged them not to give up, insisting that there were other excellent, high-profile lawyers who might take on the case simply because of its growing publicity. But her enthusiasm was as strained as their polite attention.

She was saying good-bye when the roar of a powerful car engine drowned out her voice. Someone had pulled up outside. They all turned toward the door as if some magnetic force had drawn them. The shaman smiled, and Honor's nerves leaped in anticipation. Could it be Johnny?

Her astonishment that it might be him was mixed with apprehension. If he'd come to offer his help, it was an answered prayer. But his anger was so vivid in her mind, she could imagine any number of other frightening motives. She'd suggested he avenge himself against her father. Was that was he wanted? Or was it she he'd come after?

The door swung open.

Johnny stepped over the threshold to murmurs of shock and excitement. Honor reached out as if to steady herself and caught hold of nothing but thin air. No one else in the room had seen him in person in eighteen years. But to her he looked so fundamentally different from the attorney with the expensively tailored suits and the modern office that she had to tell herself he wasn't a figment of her imagination.

He wore faded jeans with patches on the legs, a black T-shirt, and a buckskin vest. With his long hair flying free under the strip of rawhide tied around his forehead, he looked as Apache as anyone in the room.

An Apache on the warpath, Honor thought. The hostile lines of his handsome jaw spelled out trouble, and as he approached the group, Honor stepped aside, immensely relieved when he walked up to his grandfather rather than to her. He had the newspaper article she'd given him in his hand, and he held it up for the old man to see.

"Who's representing this boy?" he asked. "I'd like to speak with his counsel."

The young attorney spoke up. "No one's been retained yet. I'm here from the Indian Legal Services to review the matter. It's possible I'll be taking the case."

"Then I'll talk to you," Johnny said.

The shaman raised his hand to intervene. "Why are you here?" he asked Johnny.

Johnny's gaze flashed angrily over the crowd and settled on Honor. "I don't want to see another Apache kid get burned at the stake. I'm here to make sure that doesn't happen."

Sighs of relief could be heard, and even Honor relaxed slightly. But the shaman didn't seem to be satisfied, and the tension rose again as he and Johnny faced each other. The old man's response to Johnny's announcement was a stoic nod. There would be no apologies between two such proud men, Honor realized. Neither would acknowledge the rift between them, or even the blood ties that bound them.

"The boy's situation is only a symptom," the shaman said. "We must fight the disease. Will you take our case against the mining company?"

Johnny hesitated, reluctant to get himself any more deeply entangled than he already was. "It's not that simple," he explained. "Technically in a case like this, both the secretary of the interior and the commissioner of Indian Affairs have to approve the attorney. There's some red tape involved, but I've got contacts, and I'll do what I can to expedite things."

"Good," the old man said, "that's good."

"In the meantime I can provide legal assistance and help prepare the case."

"Yes," the shaman said emphatically. "You must prepare as if for battle, your mind, your body, your spirit."

Johnny wasn't sure what the old man was getting at, but he didn't like the sound of it. "There'll be a tremendous amount of work involved," he said, ignoring the remark. "I'll want to talk to whoever's been working on the case, and I'll need a support team for the research—"

"Anyone can read law books and do research," the shaman said, cutting him off. "We have legal-aid agencies for that. This is a battle for our right to pursue our livelihood, to protect our sovereignty as a tribe, and you are a proven warrior in the legal arena. But you must think like an Apache if you're going to fight for Apaches."

"What are you saying?" Johnny asked.

"You must go to the white mountains, where the spirits reside. You must find the medicine that will invoke your power."

A vein in Johnny's forehead began to tighten and throb. Since the trial he had done everything possible to separate himself from tribal customs, and

especially from the ancient mysticism that his grandfather was steeped in. "If I take this case, I have to
fight it my way."

"Your way is not powerful enough. You must listen
to the spirits, consult the four winds."

Johnny couldn't hide his exasperation. "My way is
powerful enough to have won nearly every important
case I've argued, all the way up to the state supreme
court. Somehow I managed all that without consult-
ing the four winds."

"Those were not Indian matters."

"Why the hell do you want me to take on your case
if you object to my methods?"

The old man persisted as though he were trying to
reason with a child. "It isn't me who wants you. It's
the spirits. When they call, our first duty is to listen."

Johnny shook his head. He was getting very close
to the end of his rope. "I'm already questioning my
sanity just by being here. All I need now is to start
listening to spirits."

The shaman turned his back on Johnny and spoke
to the tribal leader in hushed tones. After a moment
he swung around to face Johnny again. "You're free
to go."

"What? You're firing me?"

"Only a fool would hire an attorney who can't win."

Johnny raised his hands, his eyes flashing hotly
over Honor as he did so. *If it weren't for her—* He
stopped himself in the middle of the caustic thought.
She wasn't the cause of his trouble with the tribe.
That had started with his birth. His quarrel with his
grandfather had to do with beliefs and superstitions
so arcane he didn't know how to address them,
much less fight them. But Honor was the reason he'd
left the tribe. And she was part of the reason he was
back here now, a large part of it.

"All right," he said at last, speaking to the front
door as though it were his sworn enemy. "I'll go to the
mountains, if that's what you want."

"It's not what I want," the shaman replied.

Johnny spun around to face his grandfather. "I said I'll go, but I have a condition."

"What is that?"

"It involves her." He indicated Honor. "I'd like to speak to her privately."

Honor felt as if the attention of the entire room had shifted to her. She met the shaman's silent, watchful gaze, but found no guidance there. Turning to Johnny's smoldering heat, she felt a pool of liquid weakness in the pit of her stomach. Lord, but she was a fool for love where he was concerned. She had no backbone at all. "All right," she said.

Johnny walked to the front door of the building and opened it, waiting for her.

Once outside, Honor walked to the shade of a large aspen where a black-and-silver Jeep Cherokee was parked. By the way Johnny leaned up against the car's chassis, facing her, his arms loosely folded, she was sure it must be the car he'd driven.

The very casualness of his stance made her nervous. He looked like a man who'd calculated the odds and knew he couldn't lose. "What do you want to talk about?" she asked.

"Your immediate future. Don't make any plans, because I want you here, in Whiteriver, at my beck and call."

"Why? What help could I possibly be?"

"I'm going to need an assistant—a gofer, a girl Friday, and an all-around flunky."

"I don't think I like the job description."

"Then call it whatever you want. Indentured servitude, slave labor. I'm easy."

Honor could hardly believe that he was serious. Staring at him in surprise, she had a fleeting fantasy of walking over and slapping his arrogantly handsome face. The thought gave her such intense pleasure, she savored it for a moment and felt her fingers twitch. "Why would I agree to anything like that?"

"Because you're the one who got me here, and if you want to keep me here, you'll do whatever I ask."

"Whatever you ask?"

Johnny felt a second's pleasure at her trembling intake of air. He pushed away from the car, rising to his full height, which forced her to look up to meet his gaze. He could imagine her turmoil, he could almost feel it, but he told himself he didn't care. He was calling the shots now.

"*Anything?*" she pressed, her voice faint.

Yes, he thought, probing the misty veil of her blue eyes. *Whatever I ask, Honor. Anything. Everything. And don't think I won't demand it all. Your body, your heart, whatever you hold most precious. I'll take it all and leave you just what you left me. Nothing.*

"The work will be hell," he said, letting her draw her own conclusions about what that work might be. "So make your decision carefully. Once you commit, there's no way out."

Honor turned away from him. The weakness she'd felt earlier washed through her in waves. The shaman had told her that bringing Johnny back was the way to free herself, but she wasn't free. She was hopelessly ensnared. Even if she wanted to resist him, she couldn't. The Apache boy's freedom was at stake. From now until this nightmare was over, she was hostage to Johnny's every whim, his darkest fantasies.

Six

A huge ceremonial bonfire blazed in the old fairgrounds down by the river. The flames leaped high,
showering the darkness with white-hot sparks and
making ghosts of the plumes of smoke that drifted
into the night. Residents came from every corner of
the reservation, drawn by the primordial beauty of
the fire, the chanting of tribal medicine men, and the
sensual throb of rawhide drums.

Honor sat among the crowd, aware of the mounting tension around her. Tonight the *gaan* dancers
would perform what some still called "the devil
dance." Costumed to represent the *gaan*, which were
believed to be ancient mountain spirits who resided
in sacred caves, the dancers would drive away evil
spirits and invoke blessings on the tribe's endeavors
and on Johnny as a strong and able warrior.

The drums ceased, and a hush fell over the crowd
as the tribal leaders filed into the fairgrounds and
took their places around the roaring fire. The first to
enter were the representatives of the neighboring
districts, all considered to be honored guests. Next
came the White Mountain tribal leaders, led by the
tall, weathered man Honor had met that day. In the
ritual dances of the past the tribe's warriors always

entered last, after the others were seated. Tonight the last person to enter the arena was Johnny.

Honor's breath caught when she saw him.

He was naked except for a breechcloth and calf-high moccasins, and as he walked toward the fire, its roaring light turned his bronze skin to molten gold. The flames that danced over his muscular torso seemed to caress him, stroking him with the sensuality of a woman's touch. And his hair spilled like glittering black water over his powerful shoulders.

It was not a sight Honor was in any way prepared for. And neither was she expecting to see him painted with stark slashes of black and white pigment. The streaks on his face and body evoked memories of the Apache warriors who fought in the bloody Indian wars of the prior century.

He moved with the same animal grace she'd witnessed in the courtroom, and as he took his place next to the tribal leader, the drums and chanting grew louder, turning feverish. Torches could be seen approaching the bonfire from the darkness beyond. The medicine men's chanting shrilled to an eerie, high-pitched wail, and suddenly the *gaan* dancers appeared, swooping out of the night like devils. Their faces were concealed by black hoods, and the huge spiked crowns they wore were vibrantly painted with sacred Apache symbols—sunlike spheres, lightning bolts, and snakes with forked tails.

The five dancers approached the fire and backed off, melting in and out of the darkness several times before one of them broke loose and burst out of the shadows, dashing through the crowd, whirling a bull-roarer. The drums rose to a fever pitch, and the other dancers materialized again, encircling Johnny.

The *gaan* leader carried a triple medicine cross adorned with feathers, which he offered to Johnny, jerking it back as Johnny reached for it. The chanting soared to an eerie shriek, and the crowd shouted Apache words that Honor couldn't understand. She suddenly felt afraid, as if this were some test Johnny must pass.

The leader coaxed and taunted Johnny until the din grew unbearable. At last, with a dramatic flourish, he touched the crown of Johnny's head with his medicine cross, then brought the wand to his own mouth and released a hissing breath.

The crowd gasped as Johnny sprang up unexpectedly, his muscles rippling with firelight, his hair aglow. The chanters shrieked a warning, and the dancers swarmed around him, slicing the air with their wands as though fighting off demons. One of the wands struck Johnny's arm, another his chest, lacerating his skin. Honor watched in horror, but Johnny didn't move to protect himself in any way. He didn't even flinch at the blows. As the dancers hissed and leaped, Honor was reminded of an exorcism, and she couldn't help wondering if the evil they were trying to ward off was associated with Johnny's birth.

The bizarre ceremony went on until all five *gaan* dancers had performed rituals that were both beautiful and grotesque over Johnny's statuelike form. After each dance, Chy Starhawk, as chief medicine man, offered sacred pollen to the four winds, then showered Johnny with the golden powder.

Honor was hypnotized by what she saw. Johnny remained unmoving as the medicine cross was applied to various parts of his body. He looked as much a magical, supernatural creature as the dancers. With his eyes lit by the fire and his body dusted with gold, he appeared eerily capable of invoking powers, including the powers of darkness. She knew the ceremony might go on all night, until all the evil spirits had been driven away and the *gaan*'s benevolence was assured. But she couldn't tear herself away from the primal power of it.

In the morning Johnny would leave for the mountains on foot, wearing only what he wore now, with no provisions or weapons except what he could forage from nature. The shaman had told Honor that she was to be involved in some way with Johnny's ordeal, but he'd refused to tell her how. That possibility had intrigued her at first. Now it was beginning to alarm her.

Honor woke up with a start, sensing the presence of someone in her darkened motel room. She lay very still, hardly daring to breathe as she became aware of a shadowy figure hovering near the foot of the bed. Somehow she found the button at the base of table lamp next to her bed and pressed it.

The sudden burst of light blinded her, revealing the intruder as a black-on-white form, like a foreground figure in a photographic negative. She shielded her eyes, trying to bring him into focus. Gradually the form materialized into a man.

"How did you get in here?" she asked, clutching the blankets around her as she sat up. It was Chy Starhawk who stood at the foot of her bed.

The shaman lifted a shoulder, conveying the naturalness of the situation. "The lock on your door doesn't work."

"But you can't just walk into people's room and frighten them half to death! Why didn't you knock?"

"It would have been rude to knock when you were sleeping," he explained. "I would have disturbed you."

The man's logic confounded her. But what confounded her even more was that in some impenetrable way it also made sense. "What do you want?" she asked.

He approached her with an envelope in hand. "Johnny's gone to the mountains. He left you these instructions."

Honor tore open the envelope and scanned the handwritten list on the yellow legal paper. The first items were instructions on how to proceed in the case with the Apache boy. The last items were more personal. "Wear your hair down," he'd printed in bold strokes. But it was the postscript that made her blush. "Anything I ask," it said, and there were three slashes under the words.

Honor glanced up at Chy Starhawk, wondering how much he knew. His darkly eloquent eyes told her he knew it all, what had happened between her and Johnny, what would happen. Not the details perhaps, but the inescapable web of emotion they'd found themselves entangled in, and the web of life that awaited them.

"When does Johnny return?" she asked.

"Only he can say," the old man answered.

Honor worked incessantly for the next few days, trying to complete all of Johnny's instructions before he came back. He'd asked her to arrange bail and secure the Apache boy's release from jail. He'd also asked her to work with the attorney from the legal-services agency in researching the case, including searching the legal record for similar incidents. And his final request was that she contact Geoff Dias, one of his former partners in the recovery work he'd done for the Pentagon. Johnny wanted Geoff to run surveillance on the mining operation and see what evidence he could find to support the tribe's claims of toxic runoff, then bring the information to Honor on the reservation.

Honor worked late into the night, poring over casebooks written in legalese she barely understood. She pushed herself until the young attorney she was working with became concerned and advised her to slow down. But the case had begun to feel like a second chance to Honor. If she could help to free the accused boy, perhaps that would in some way balance the mistakes she'd made. And it also gave her a kind of comfort to know that she and Johnny were in accord on something, that they were both working on the boy's behalf.

And yet what occupied her mind the most as she tried to immerse herself in the case was Johnny himself. Nights in the mountains were still frigid this time of year, and Johnny had no clothing, no food, no weapons to protect himself against wolves, mountain lions, and other predators. As the days passed, she found herself worrying more and more about his safety. He had Apache blood and instincts, but did he have the ability to survive such a punishing physical test?

She was working late one evening in the office she shared with the legal-services attorney when again she felt a presence in the room. As she glanced up, Johnny's grandfather moved toward her out of the shadows.

"It's time," he said. "You must join Johnny in the white mountains."

"Join him?" Honor closed the casebook she'd been reading. "Is he all right? Does he know about this?"

"He does not need to know."

"But why am I going?"

"Because you are part of the medicine through which he will find his power."

Honor couldn't hide her surprise, not only at what Chy Starhawk was suggesting, but at what he was asking her to do. It seemed as if he were casually pulling strings and manipulating people's fates without any regard to the dangers involved. "I'm sure Johnny would consider me an enemy of his power," she said softly but emphatically. "I told you before that in his heart he still hates me for what I did."

"Johnny will come to see what is so," the shaman said, seeming not to be swayed by her concerns.

"I don't think you understand," she persisted. "He wants revenge."

The old man's shrug was fatalistic. "I do understand. It was the ancient way of our people. To let a wrong go unpunished invited more wrongs. One act balanced another."

Honor rose from her chair, frightened and appalled. "And you're willing to let that happen? You're willing to send me in as some kind of human sacrifice so that Johnny can find his power, as you call it?"

"It is not I who must be willing. It is you."

"But you do believe that Johnny will try to exact his revenge?" Honor's pulse rate went wild as the shaman's silence seemed to indicate his agreement. "And that I will be hurt in all of this?" she asked.

The silence seemed to drag on forever before the shaman finally nodded, a measure of sympathy in his expression. "Yes, you surely will be hurt in all of this. But if you are brave and strong enough to endure it, you will win."

"What do you mean? Win what?"

"The right to know . . . what you do not yet know."

Honor heaved a tremulous sigh and turned away, wishing she could make the old man understand how terribly dangerous his suggestion was. To interrupt Johnny's vigil, to inflict herself upon him now, would surely trigger all the dark impulses Johnny himself had warned her about, the very rage she was trying to avoid. She wasn't brave or strong enough for that!

Johnny sat cross-legged before the glowing embers of the small campfire he'd built. The kindling crackled and popped noisily, filling the air with the rich scent of pine. Behind him a full moon was on the rise, spilling its dazzlingly bright light through a canopy of blue spruce and ponderosa pine.

The contents of his medicine bag lay scattered on the ground before him, each charm's distinctive color representing one of the four directions—black jet for East, blue turquoise for South, red stone for West, and white shell for North. His grandfather had told him that the stones would reveal secrets, but tonight their starlike patterns had begun to blur and distort before his eyes, taking on sinister shapes.

A coyote howled in the distance. Johnny glanced up at the night sky and knew it was time. He had been told to fast and let the spirits speak, but the hunger and fatigue that resulted from going several days without food were fouling his senses. The full moon meant it was time to hunt.

The knife he slipped into the top of his high moccasins was a weapon he'd worked from chalcedony, a translucent quartz stone. It was sharp enough to kill quickly and virtually painlessly, but first he had to be clever enough to ensnare the animal.

A hawk swooped out of nowhere as Johnny rose to track the coyote. Dizziness washed over him as he watched the magnificent bird dip and soar, its wings flashing silver in the moonlight. Johnny began to follow the creature on instinct, knowing it was no ordinary bird.

He moved swiftly through the trees, tracking the hawk, but as the bird soared over an alpine meadow, Johnny stopped in confusion. Hundreds of rabbits danced and bobbed in the moon-drenched meadow, weaving stuporously. At first he thought he was hallucinating, but he'd heard of this phenomenon from Apache lore, animals made drunk by moonlight. Perhaps that was why the hawk had led him there. For an easy kill.

But the bird shrieked urgently, reclaiming Johnny's attention and drawing it to a mountain stream that crashed through a stand of pines. A puma hovered on the opposite shore of the stream, its golden coat bleached white by the intense light. Johnny crouched to get his knife. When he looked up, the cat was gone, and a woman was standing in its place.

She was surreal in the moonlight, naked beneath a

gauzy, luminescent gown. Her long blond hair flowed like the water at her feet, and though her face was veiled in shadows, he knew who she was.

"Johnny," she whispered, holding out her hand to him. "Come for me." The river picked up her whispers and repeated his name, chanting it magically, sensually. Johnny knew she must be some kind of vision, but he was struck by how hauntingly lovely she was, and the way her nakedness was revealed to him in such fantastic detail.

As though aware of his fascination, she drew a hand to her breast, running her little finger over its fullness, encircling the aureole. Johnny watched, both excited and disturbed as she let her hand glide down her body. She touched herself erotically, and he began to harden.

"Deliver me," she murmured. She held out her hand again, beseechingly, almost sadly. "Johnny . . . take me, save me."

Johnny started toward her, but the river roared and grew wild. Transfixed, he watched as she waded into the turbulent water. *Johnny, take me, save me.* Her plea reverberated in his head and echoed thunderously in the rapids. The water raged, plastering the gown to her body and beating against her violently, but she kept going as though unaware of the danger.

Suddenly she sank thigh-deep in the swirling water and faltered, struggling to catch her balance. The current was deadly, and she plunged deeper, sucked into a howling vortex where the rocks were jagged and slick with moss.

"Johnny!" someone screamed. The cry echoed in the blackness above him. The hawk?

The woman reached out to him in desperation as the turbulence dragged her down. Her broken whisper was torn away by the thunderous currents. "Johnny . . . forgive me."

Johnny plunged into the river, the water beating at

him as he caught hold of her arms. Adrenaline spiked his heart rate. He fought to pull her out of the whirlpool, trying to drag her toward him. With a roar of rage he pulled her free. But as he lifted her into his arms, he saw her anguish. A brilliant glitter of tears flowed into the water droplets on her face.

It wasn't until he reached the shore with her limp body that he realized he must have been hallucinating. The woman was Honor, but she wearing a traditional Apache camp dress, not a luminescent gown. And though she was wearing her hair down, it had been drawn loosely into a single braid.

The night air had a sharp bite to it as he headed back to camp with his sodden burden. He broke into a jog, knowing he had to get her out of the cold. She was semiconscious and shuddering violently. By the time he reached the sheltering copse of pine and spruce where he'd spent the last several days, the fire had nearly died out.

He settled her in the primitive lean-to he'd rigged together from tree branches and leaves, then set about building up the fire. Her wet clothing had to come off, he told himself, but he had nothing dry to cover her with and no inclination whatsoever to undress a woman who'd already given him a world of grief with her clothes on.

Moments later, bending over her huddled form, he realized he couldn't even give her his own clothes. He had none. He couldn't see any visible injuries on her body, but she could easily die of exposure alone.

His conscience worked at him as the night wore on and the temperature dropped. Between her convulsive tremors and his own experience with the freezing conditions at night, he finally talked himself into removing her voluminous skirt. The damp cotton fabric resisted him, clinging to her skin and tangling up in his hands as he tried to peel it away. With a soft curse he gave up trying not to touch her. His fingers pressed into her flesh, sending a shudder through him as he worked the material loose and stripped it away from her body.

As he tugged the fabric over her moccasined feet, she made a sound and drew her legs up, curling into a fetal position. Reluctantly aware of the transparent wet panties she wore, of the tantalizing curve of buttock he'd exposed, Johnny couldn't stop himself from looking at her, or from wanting her.

Something rose wildly inside him—animal lust or longing. Whatever it was, the flash of desire hit him so hard, it took his breath away before he had it under control. The position she'd curled into conjured images of the most erotic kind of lovemaking possible. He imagined himself lifting her hair and kissing the nape of her neck, caressing her naked legs and cupping the rounds of her buttocks in his palms. He imagined how hard he would be as he fitted his body to the luscious curve of hers.

How hard he was now!

Desire slammed into him again, a blunt force. She was leaving in the morning, he told himself. However she'd managed to get here, she was going back the same way

He held her skirt over the fire, shaking it until it was warm and dry enough to provide her with some protection. Less erotic questions took over his concerns as he covered her with the warmed material. He couldn't imagine what she was doing up here, unless she'd been sent to bring him news about the case.

His hunger forgotten, he sat through the night, feeding the fire and waiting until her moans and shudders gave way. Finally she sank into a heavy sleep, and he closed his eyes in relief, thinking to catch a moment's rest. Within seconds he'd drifted in a haze of exhaustion. . . .

The chatter of mockingbirds brought him to with a start. He couldn't remember where he was or what had happened until he glanced around and saw

Honor still sleeping in the lean-to. Dawn was breaking over the hills, painting the jagged crests with a rich silvery light. In a few more moments the mountains would be awake, alive.

He'd fallen asleep sitting up, and the muscles of his thighs screamed in protest as he pushed to his feet. An animal growl vibrated in his throat as he stretched the kinks out of his body, taking pleasure in the heat and energy that seeped back into his muscles and dissipated the aching stiffness. The next sensation that hit him was hunger, ravenous hunger.

The earth smelled fresh and fertile. Night had left a veil of moisture on the forest's verdant undergrowth. He glanced around, knowing there wasn't time to hunt game. He'd been given various tests of strength to pass before he could return to Whiteriver, including scaling the mountain's highest peak where the *gaan* were thought to reside in their sacred caves. He'd planned to do that today, and he needed an early start. He would have to go in search of food—roots, berries, nuts, anything that was edible.

When Johnny returned to the camp an hour later, Honor was stirring, as though about to wake up. Much of her heavy blond hair had pulled loose from its braid, and she looked tousled and beautiful, a princess coming awake after a century's sleep. He was standing over her as she opened her eyes, wishing she didn't make him ache like that moonstruck young kid who had worshiped at her feet, wishing he didn't still harbor such volatile feelings.

Honor blinked to clear her fuzzy vision, and as the dusky-skinned man above her gradually came into focus, she told herself to say something intelligible, like good morning. She couldn't manage words, however. Not even something that basic. It was more than physical weakness stopping her, it was the impact of Johnny himself. He wore a scarlet sash around his head in traditional Apache style, and a medicine cord hung from his neck. Other than that, and the moccasins and the G-string he called a loincloth, he was as naked as the night he'd stood before the fire at the fairgrounds.

"How are you feeling?" he asked.

"I don't know yet." She was aware of a general soreness, but nothing that might indicate a serious injury. "I'm afraid to move and find out."

"Think you could eat?" He held up the leather pouch he'd filled with pine nuts, wild berries, and roots.

"I'll give it my best."

He knelt to help her sit up, and the warmth of his arms and hands supporting her felt wonderful. Suddenly she knew what was different about him! He wasn't scowling. He looked more concerned than angry.

"Be careful," he said as the cotton skirt slid off her legs. "You haven't got much on under there."

She lifted the material, glanced at her bare legs, and lowered it just as quickly. "You did this?"

"Don't make it sound like an act of perversion. I was trying to keep you from catching pneumonia."

He was still touching her arm as if to steady her, but Honor was only aware of the slow burn of his fingers against her skin. He seemed to brand her in some way every time he touched her. The position he'd crouched in made the muscles of his thighs stand out, and no matter which way she looked, there seemed to be brawny arms and legs to contend with. Having him up close and unclothed made her more than a little uncomfortable.

"Maybe we could have some of that food you mentioned," she suggested.

He helped her get settled more comfortably, then opened the leather pouch and handed it to her. "Help yourself," he said. "It's the closest thing to fast food we're going to get up here."

Honor reached into the bag and scooped out a

handful of what could have been trail mix, except it had blackberries instead of raisins. She chewed the concoction slowly, aware of the stringy toughness of the roots and the tart snap of the unripe berries.

Johnny took a handful, too, then several more. She quickly had her fill, but he wolfed down about half of the bag's contents before he stopped to ask her how and why she came to be there.

"Your grandfather could answer better than I can," she said. "He told me it was time I joined you in the mountains. I argued with him, but he isn't easily swayed, as you know. I was brought up here on horseback by a man from the tribe, dropped off by the river, and told to wait there for you."

"Wait for me at the river? How would anyone have known I was going to be there?"

"How does your grandfather know anything? He has a sixth sense. I'm convinced of it."

Johnny didn't share her certainty, and he wasn't at all happy with what his grandfather had done. "You nearly drowned in that river," he said, remembering her cries and his own confusion. He'd thought she was a hallucination at first. What if he'd walked away and let her drown? The thought made him sick inside. Fear and anger welled up in the pit of his stomach, mixing with a sense of frustration at the things he couldn't control. *What if she had died?*

"I don't know what the old man has in mind," he said roughly, pushing to his feet. "But you can't stay here. You'll be dead from exposure or eaten by wolves before the week is out."

"I can't go back," she said. "Not by myself. I'd never find the way."

Johnny swept up the leather pouch and attached its rawhide ties to the waistband of his loincloth. She'd never find her way back to Whiteriver, and he couldn't take her there now, not without going up against his grandfather again. "In that case you're going to be stuck here alone. All day, maybe the night too. I'm climbing the peak this morning, and I don't know when I'll get back."

She started to rise, hesitating as the skirt slid off her legs. Her eyes emanated desperation. "Take me with you," she said.

"No, that's out of the question. You'd never make it." God, but she tugged at him with her soft yearnings. She pulled at his gut, his heart, every damn vital organ in his body. "You're not exactly dressed to scale cliffs," he said, regarding her clothing with barely veiled contempt. "That skirt would end up wrapped around your neck."

"That's not a problem. I can shorten it." She pulled the skirt off, apparently intending to begin her alterations immediately. "Look, I'll rip off the bottom tier."

Johnny took a deep breath and sent up a prayer to the gods of willpower. She didn't seem to have any idea that she'd just exposed most of herself to his eyes—silk panties, hips, and bare, shapely legs. Everything but her breasts, he thought grimly, and that was probably coming next if he complained about the blouse she was wearing.

"You're *not* coming with me." His gaze was scathingly hot as he raked it over her body, climbing up her naked limbs to the startled expression on her flushed face. "We have a deal, remember? You agreed to do what I ask. Anything I ask. So if you don't want me to start asking right now, then you'd be wise to cover yourself up and quit arguing."

She set her jaw as though fighting a wild desire to defy him. "That will teach me to make deals with arrogant bastards," she mumbled, yanking the skirt over her legs.

Johnny's faint smile revealed none of the hunger that was building inside him. His blood was rushing, pooling in dark male places. One day soon he was going to take her up on their deal. He was going to ask, and she was going to give. Anything he wanted. *Everything she had.* He wouldn't be satisfied with anything less. One day soon, he told himself.

Seven

"A fresh kill," Johnny murmured, kneeling for a closer look at the carcass he'd found on the bank of the creek he'd been following for the past half hour. The animal wasn't much bigger than a large rodent, probably a pack rat, and it was unlikely that the predator who'd killed it had satisfied its hunger with such a meager meal. There was a good chance the big animal was still in the area, still hunting.

Johnny touched the top of his moccasin, reassuring himself his knife was still there. He would have to stay on guard. Perhaps the puma he'd seen the night before hadn't been a hallucination. But even if it was, there were plenty of other predators known to inhabit the area, including wolves and bobcats.

He scanned the woods around him and rose to continue his climb. The rock-studded creek provided a natural clearing and a ready source of fresh water, but the trail ahead presented a problem. The babbling brook turned into steep cliffs and a spectacular waterfall. He would have to take a detour through the trees.

He stopped for a moment in the dark, cool shade of the forest, breathing in the earth's natural, fertile musk. The smells triggered memories of the more pleasant aspects of his early childhood, when he would escape to the hills and pretend that the Apache still ruled these mountain, forests, and rivers with the same freedom they had in earlier times. As a boy, he'd taken pride in the fact that the Apache were the fiercest warriors in the Indian wars, subdued only because the white soldiers had pitted Apaches against each other. In many cases captive warriors were turned into scouts and forced to search out their own kind, the "invisible enemy" hiding in these very mountains.

A rustle of leaves pricked Johnny's senses, bringing him out of his reverie. He went still. Even if an animal had picked up his scent, it wouldn't see him unless he moved. The faint sounds were coming from behind him, from lower down the slope, and he thought they were made by a surefooted cat moving through the brush. Humans were clumsy and noisy.

As the rustling continued, nearing him, he drew his knife and turned into the trunk of a huge spruce. He crouched soundlessly. The forest was dark and mysterious, alive with shadows. It was difficult to see, but if the animal was close enough and Johnny was quick enough, he could come from behind and sever its jugular before it even sensed his presence.

His heart was pumping in quick, hard jerks. This was the first time he'd used his military training since he stopped doing recovery work for the Pentagon, and the adrenaline that had flowed through his veins then was surging now. He quieted his mind and his senses, listening, waiting.

His knife blade glinted, hit by a laser of sunlight.

A tree branch snapped explosively.

Johnny lunged as a shadowy form moved into his line of sight. He knocked it off balance with a body blow and pinned it to the ground with his weight. Reacting out of instinct more than training, he grabbed a fistful of hair and jerked the creature's head back, pressing the knife blade to its soft throat.

Soft throat?

His hand froze as he realized he had a human being underneath him, a female human being! He sat up and rolled her over roughly, quickly, without releasing her. The knife that was locked in his fist still hovered near her throat.

Johnny's blood roared through his veins as he stared down at Honor's terror-stricken expression. "I could have killed you," he said, his voice trembling with fury and disbelief. "I was a muscle twitch away from killing you!"

She was rigid with fear, apparently unable to speak.

Johnny was astonished at the violence coursing through him. He could barely control the impulse he felt to shake her senseless, to punish her with all the brutality in his soul for her idiocy in coming up behind him that way. It enraged him to think that she would have taken such a risk.

"What are you doing here?" he asked.

She shook her head, apparently unable or unwilling to speak with the knife blade at her throat. He kept it there anyway. To hell with what she wanted. The only perverse satisfaction he got from this woman was in frightening her, and that was damn little compensation for the horror she'd just put him through.

Straddling her, he brought her arms over her head and locked her wrists to the ground with one hand. Adrenaline was still pounding through him as he bent low over her body, pinning her down with his forearm, his face inches from hers. The knife was right where he wanted it, at her pale, trembling throat.

"I asked you a question," he said, his voice a menacing whisper. "What are you doing here?"

She spoke with great effort, her voice so hoarse she couldn't finish the sentence. "Th-there's a mountain lion—"

"Mountain lion? Where?"

"D-down at the camp. I couldn't stay there."

"Why the hell didn't you yell or do something to get my attention?"

"I couldn't." She swallowed against the knife blade. "I was afraid to yell for fear it would attract the cat. I found your trail along the creek and followed it. Then I lost you."

A tremor shook her body as Johnny drew the knife back slightly. Her throat caught in a dry sob of relief, and she began to shudder like a woman snatched from certain death. Johnny knew it was a delayed reaction to the horror of what had nearly happened, but he didn't release her. Nor did he apologize for his fury, even though it was clear she hadn't been playing games or trying to catch him off guard.

She moved beneath him, her hips bumping the inside of his thighs. "Can I get up now?" she asked.

"Yes," he said, but he didn't move. He'd suddenly become aware of the shape of her body beneath his, the warmth. He could feel the deepening beat of her heart and the thrust of her breasts against his bare chest. As more and more signals began to fire in his brain, he realized the arm he was holding her down with was pressed against the side of her breast, nestled into its melting fullness. At that moment nothing on God's earth could have induced him to move.

He told himself to get up, to break the physical connection before it was too late. If he'd meant to scare her, he'd done it. If he'd meant to teach her an object lesson, he'd done that too. She would never creep up behind him again. There was no reason in hell for him to keep her pinned to the ground underneath him. No reason except that he wanted her that way.

He wondered angrily how she could be so beautiful when she was such a mess. Twigs and leaves were caught in her hair, and soil smudged her face. But

he was as drawn to her dishevelment now as he had
been to her dreamy perfection years ago. His heart
began to thud noticeably. He wanted to taste the
sooty marks near her chin, the dirt on her lips. He
wanted to kiss her until they both forgot who they
were and where they were.

"Johnny?" she said as he bent toward her.

He caught himself a second before their lips met,
caught himself like a drunk about to fall off the
wagon. He cursed, his voice edged with disbelief.
"This is no way to be climbing a mountain."

She flushed and moved beneath him again. "I've
never had a conversation at knife-point either. Except with you."

He glanced at the weapon in his hand, heaved a
sigh, and stuck the blade in the ground.

"Are you going to let me up now?" she asked.

"I don't think so," he answered, quite truthfully.

She smelled subtly of violets, moss, and river
mists. He might have been picking up the scents
around him and attributing them to her, except that
he remembered those same scents from their youth.
She had always smelled that way. And the river had
always been her favorite place for secret meetings.

Memories began to filter through his consciousness, glimmers of their walks by the water's edge, the
creaky wooden footbridge they'd once braved, the
calico kitten they'd rescued from a sycamore tree.
Honor had wanted to keep the kitten, but her father
wouldn't permit it.

"You were a strange kid," he said, knowing better
that to open up their past to conversation. "You
always insisted on taking off your shoes and wading
in the river as if it were some kind of ritual. Why did
you do that?"

"I don't know. Probably the same reason you were
always skipping stones across the water."

"But I had a good reason for skipping stones. I was
into intellectual pursuits."

She began to laugh, and the sound of it was so infectious, he found himself smiling. She searched his face with her eyes, as if she were trying to remember what had gone wrong between them. "How I missed you after you left," she said suddenly, her voice full of heartache. "I couldn't talk to anyone but you. No one understood."

He felt as if she'd taken his own knife and pierced him through the heart with it. *No one understood.* She could have stolen those words from some dark, mangled place inside of him. As a kid, he'd fantasized that he and Honor were exactly alike except for the shade of their skin, that they shared the same pain and fears. Two misfits, two kindred souls. It was a simple thing, pure. They were friends. She understood him, and she was the only one who ever had. That was what made what she'd done so damn unbearable, so unforgivable.

The pain inside him twisted like a serrated blade, turning in the most tender part of his heart. It was beyond his ability to control, or to endure. With a harsh sound he pushed away from her and sprang to his feet. He wrenched his knife from the ground, and not knowing what else to do, he fired it at the nearest tree, grimacing as it stuck fast.

If she'd meant to give him an object lesson, she had. This was why he couldn't dwell in the past, why he couldn't let himself get close to her. Why he shouldn't even be on the same mountain with her!

"My test isn't this mountain," he said. "It's you, Honor. My grandfather sent you because he knew if anything could defeat me, it would be you. Like some demented sorcerer, that old man reached into the darkest part of my soul and pulled out my worst nightmare."

He walked to the tree and freed the knife, sheathing it in the buckskin cuff of his moccasin. "Now I'm going to climb this mountain," he said savagely. "And I don't give a damn what you do, as long as you stay out of my way. If you cross my path again, you'll be crying bitter tears."

Honor pushed to her elbow and watched him start up the forested incline. Bastard, she thought, choking off a throaty sob. Anger churned inside her, the heat of it overriding all her other emotions, even her fear of him. Every time their past came into the conversation, he turned into a snarling beast. But she hadn't brought it up this time, he had!

She struggled to her feet, dusted off the blue chintz camp dress she'd altered, and started up the same rise he'd taken. Her movements were stiff, her gait awkward from aching muscles and the sting of abrasions. She was bruised and scraped from being knocked to the ground, but she wasn't going back to camp and lick her wounds like a whipped dog. That was an option she wouldn't even consider.

The outrage simmering inside her had been building for days. She was damn tired of being threatened with knives, insulted on a regular basis, and blamed for everything that had ever happened in Johnny's miserable life. She was more than willing to take responsibility for her mistakes, but he couldn't even discuss the situation rationally.

She continued climbing, shoving away the branches that snagged at her clothing as she tried to find her way back to the creek. To hell with him, she thought. Despite what he might think, the mountain was plenty big enough for both of them, and she intended to climb it too. It wasn't just about proving to him that she could do it, although she wanted that satisfaction badly. It was a personal thing, she realized, an inner call to arms, as if she were mobilizing to do battle with her own fears and insecurities.

She didn't question the wisdom of a woman in her unremarkable physical condition trying to make such a difficult climb. She had more immediate problems to worry about, such as not getting hopelessly lost in the woods and dying of exposure, as

Johnny had predicted. Fortunately he'd left her a crude trail to follow with the broken branches and undergrowth he'd cut away. And when that trail led her back to the creek, she was greatly relieved. She even got a glimpse of him once, well ahead of her and moving nimbly alongside the rushing water, his powerful body gleaming in the sun, the red bandanna glowing against his black hair.

The sight was enough to make her stop and watch silently until he'd disappeared from view. He'd looked like an incarnation of the warriors and prophets who had roamed the Arizona landscape a century ago, Cochise and his son Natchez, even the dreaded outlaw Geronimo.

Johnny was as magnificent as they were in some physical way, and he was also as unpredictable and dangerous, she reminded herself, resuming her own assault on the mountain. As she followed the seemingly endless path of the creek, she began to appreciate the cool shade of the forest, especially as the air grew thinner and the sun hotter. Her breathing quickly became labored, and she had to stop frequently. The icy creek water she splashed on her flushed face cooled the heat temporarily, but the way the sun was bearing down, she knew it must be burning her to a crisp. Her calves and thighs ached with a fatigue that made her want to moan aloud.

Eventually she was slowed to a halting pace, reduced to the concentrated mental effort of putting one foot in front of the other. As every fiber of her willpower was drawn into that painful process, she began to realize she wasn't going to make it. She wasn't a trained climber, or even a hiker. She wasn't used to the altitude.

Somehow she kept going, one leaden step at a time, until finally the exaggerated slowness of her progress began to develop into a rhythm that was almost meditative. The screaming muscles in her legs went silent, numbed by overuse, yet lifting and falling as though on automatic pilot. Her respiration dropped to a level so instinctive she hardly seemed to be breathing at all, and still she kept on.

Johnny splashed his face with cold water from the creek, then cupped another handful and drank deeply. He shook his hands, dried them on his bare legs, and rose, glancing down the clearing. There was no sign of her and hadn't been for some time.

He wasn't surprised she hadn't made it this far. White Mountain was a killer of men, not to mention foolhardy debutantes. When Johnny was living among the Apache, he could remember plenty of weekend warriors who'd thought to brave the mountain's face and who'd been quickly brought to their knees. He'd been running several miles a week since his military service, but he had no altitude training, and he was feeling the effects of the climb himself.

The last mountain he'd conquered had been one of the peaks of the Andes range in Peru over six years ago. He'd been on a recovery mission to liberate some Americans taken hostage by Peruvian guerrillas. During the mission one of his partners, Geoff Dias, was taken captive by the rebels, and it had fallen to Johnny to rescue Geoff. Fortunately he'd succeeded.

The memory reminded him that Honor was supposed to have contacted Geoff about some surveillance work. Aware that he might be seeing his buddy again soon, he turned and gazed up, calculating the pitch of the steep rise ahead of him. It culminated in a very nearly vertical sheet of granite that would have to be scaled. Worse, a rock slide had all but obliterated the trail. Honor would never make it, he realized as he began to plan his own ascent up the cliff. She couldn't possibly.

He glanced back down the trail, torn. Should he head for the peak? Or play Saint Bernard to a debutante? God, how he wanted to forget she existed and finish his climb. He wanted to forget the woman's existence, period. But he didn't have it in him to leave anyone stranded on a mountainside with a hungry mountain lion on the loose. Damn her anyway. He was going to have to rescue her and take her back to camp.

He hadn't gone more than fifty feet down the trail when he spotted a blue speck coming up. He halted in disbelief, waiting until he could see the climber more clearly. He was looking for some evidence of long blond hair when he realized that it was Honor. She'd draped the blue chintz tier from her skirt over her head like a veil, and she was laboring badly, but she kept going, inching up the mountain. She looked like Mother Teresa! A very young and beautiful Mother Teresa, but the martyred saint aspect was definitely there.

He ducked back into the cover of a pine tree when she glanced up. Just his luck to get caught playing the noble savage after having made an issue about her not crossing his path. The absurdity of the situation struck him as he brought his forearm to his temple and wiped the sweat from his brow. He seemed to have some inborn, obsessive need to protect her, when he was the one who needed protection. From her! He'd come to her rescue in high school and been tried, convicted, and crucified for his trouble. Maybe one day he would learn from his mistakes.

Soundlessly he turned and began to climb again.

Tears began to roll down Honor's face as she stared at the rock slide that blocked the trail. Tears she didn't even know she was crying until she reached up and touched her cheek. A hoarse sound that might have been a sob choked her throat.

She had reached the point where pain was the sole focus of her awareness. It hurt her to move, to breathe. She couldn't draw in the air she desperately needed to keep going without feeling as if she were scalding her throat and lungs. Her lips were cracked and her tongue swollen. She couldn't even swallow without experiencing a raw, burning sensation.

Whatever the limits of her endurance were, she'd pushed past them long ago. Never in her life had she been so beaten down by fatigue, so whipped by physical pain. Nausea roiled in the pit of her stomach, undoubtedly from the effects of too little oxygen. The cramps in her leg muscles had coiled into knots. She wanted to stop, to collapse into a heap and never move again. She had the most bizarre and satisfying fantasy of decomposing into the earth and coming back as a flower or a sprig of mountain laurel, but her body wouldn't let her drop. It kept her upright; it drove her on.

One last tear rolled down her cheek.

She stared at the rocky ledge, having no idea how she was going to get up it except to do what she'd been doing, putting one foot in front of another. Gathering up her full cotton skirt, she tied it in a knot at her hip and began to work her way through the rubble of the rock slide. The boulders' jagged edges cut into her rawhide moccasins, bruising the tender soles of her feet and throwing her off balance.

As the hill steepened, she dropped to all fours, using her hands for balance and her feet for leverage. Her legs trembled with fatigue as she struggled to get a foothold on the steep ledge and then grabbed for a rock above her, dragging herself up. Exhaustion made her clumsy, but she found another chink and planted her foot again, heaving herself up to the next rock and the next. Tears flowed down her cheeks, but she forced herself to keep going, even when her leg muscles began to spasm and the jutting granite cut her pale flesh like knives.

The pain was debilitating as she inched toward the top. She was shaking so violently, it was all she could do not to let go and drop to the ground, thirty feet below. She had a flash of broken bones and multiple contusions, but she couldn't imagine hurting more than she hurt now. Sobbing out a curse word, she caught hold of a spindly pine branch and nearly snapped it in half as she hauled herself up. The next lunge brought her within a few feet of the top.

Moments later, with a hoarse cry, she pulled herself onto the rocky plateau and crumpled to her knees, head bowed. Nausea swept her in waves. She was limp and quaking, unable to move, but somehow, despite the physical upheaval of her body, she knew she'd made it. She had climbed that damn ledge.

She tried to get up, but the ground felt as though it were shifting beneath her, and she couldn't stop the terrible roiling in her stomach. A shadow dropped in front of her, and when she looked up, Johnny was there, walking across the plateau toward her. He looked like one of the *gaan*, an angry god of the mountain with the sun at his back, haloing his shoulders and torso.

She waved him away, turning her back to him as the nausea resurged. Perspiration filmed her face and neck, and a sickening rush of weakness overtook her. She swallowed in horror and bent double, dry-heaving several times before she finally retched up her breakfast of nuts and berries.

It was a ghastly, humiliating experience. She felt like a trembling mess, a helpless child who couldn't control her bodily functions. She didn't want him, of all people, to see her this way. Afterward, purged of strength, soaked in sweat, she crawled to a nearby spot in the shade of a pine tree and curled up there, trying to recover.

"You're going back," Johnny said.

"Get away from me," she pleaded.

"I'm taking you back down, dammit."

She didn't even bother to look at him. "I'm not going down," she said.

"You're going, even if I have to carry you!"

"No!" At the risk of being sick again, she raised her head defiantly. "I'm climbing to the top, and you're not stopping me. Nothing can stop me."

She waited for him to invoke their bargain, but he didn't. Instead he made a sound, like air hissing through his teeth, and Honor knew she'd surprised him. Somehow that pleased her. It almost gave her the energy to get up and continue.

"You're sick," he said. "You're bleeding, for God's sake. Look at your arm."

Honor glanced at the oozing gash on her forearm, at the cuts and bruises on her legs, and wondered why she felt no pain. Yesterday she might have fainted at the sight. Today it gave her an odd sense of strength. "I'm going on," she said, pulling the cotton veil from her head and ripping a piece from it to bandage her arm.

Moments later she was up on her feet, testing the shakiness of her legs and finding that she could actually walk. She would never have believed herself capable of such resilience. Was this what they called a second wind?

"You've got to be crazy," Johnny said harshly. "It's several more miles. You'll never make it."

Honor realized she had to get around him to get back to the trail, and for a moment she was afraid he might actually intend to stop her. Bowing her head, she began to walk in the painstakingly slow gait that had brought her this far. If the mountain couldn't conquer her, then nothing could, including him. Especially him.

"I'll make it," she said.

He wouldn't step aside as she tried to pass, and his angry stance forced her to brush up against him. His breath was hot, his body a solid wall of opposition. He felt like a force field draining off her trembling determination. She kept expecting him to do something, to grab her arm or order her to stop. When he didn't, it confused and exhausted her even more.

She managed to reach the trail, drained of energy and feeling as if she had nothing left. Somehow she kept going, but it was on nerves alone. She knew he was behind her, watching. I'll make it, she thought repeating the words like a mantra. But in her heart she was terrified he was right. She never would.

Some time later, still slogging up the steepening trail, she reached that point beyond exhaustion, beyond pain, when the mind detaches to protect itself. Fatigue had insulated her from the physical suffering, and yet on some level she knew that her lungs still caught fire with every breath she took, and her legs were so wobbly, she couldn't take a step without staggering.

She wasn't sure how long she'd been climbing, or how far she'd gone, when she noticed the darkening sky. Clouds had blocked the sun, bringing blessed coolness, but the thought of a storm alarmed her. She was above the tree line now, with no protection from the elements.

A raindrop splashed against her forearm, then several more hit her face. She kept moving, knowing if she stopped, she would collapse in a heap and never move again. She couldn't even turn her head to see if Johnny was behind her. It took too much effort, and she knew his angry countenance would throw her to the ground. It would be the straw that broke her.

Within seconds a steady, cleansing rain was falling. She took the veil from her head, letting the shower wash her face and arms. It wasn't until some time later that she gradually became aware that the steady rainfall had become a downpour, and she was soaked through to the skin. She'd fallen into a trancelike state, into that strange, deep pit of concentration that took her beyond the limits of human endurance.

Rain was pelting her as she glanced up. Wind whipped at her dress, and the clouds were thunderheads, black and roiling toward her with a paralyzing fury. She looked around, bewildered as the sky opened up with a blinding bolt of lightning. Fear struck at her heart, weakening her legs. She tried to keep moving, but nausea rose in her gorge, and a violent trembling took hold of her limbs.

The thunder cracked above her with an explosion that knocked her to her knees. It shattered what was left of her strength. She couldn't catch her breath. She couldn't even see through the downpour. Swamped by sickness and exhaustion, she curled into a fetal crouch and moaned, defeated.

"Honor?"

It was Johnny's voice. She roused, struggling to look up, but what she saw above her wasn't Johnny. It was the peak of the mountain, looming not two hundred feet away. She scrubbed the moisture from her eyes, wondering if it was an illusion. Had she come that close to reaching the top?

She felt Johnny's hand on her arm, lifting her to her feet. "No," she croaked. "*No!*" She couldn't let him help her. Not when she was so close! She began to cry in racking sobs as she fought him off and sank into a huddled mass.

"Honor, this is insane!"

"I can do it!" she shrieked.

Forcing herself to get up, she staggered up the rocky incline blindly, half crawling. Her foot came down on a sharp rock, and she screamed, dropping to all fours. She was dragging herself by the time she reached the top. Her hand outstretched, she touched the wooden post that marked the pinnacle and told its elevation, nearly twelve thousand feet. With a deep, shuddering sob of relief, she collapsed.

Lightning cracked above her. Thunder burst like a bomb.

Through a haze of rain and tears, she saw the cavelike formation of rocks beyond the post. If she could struggle a few more feet, she could make it to shelter. . . .

Her next awareness was of a crackling fire, and a storm raging hellishly outside the wall of darkness that surrounded her. She was huddled into herself, still wet to the skin and curled up against a huge boulder. Beyond the fire's healing heat, she saw Johnny sitting opposite her in the cave.

"How did I get here?" she said.

"You crawled."

"Did you help me?"

"I tried, but you wouldn't let me."

She bent her head and wept. She had done it then, without his help. She had conquered the mountain. Sobs shook her body until she couldn't cry anymore. Slumped against the boulder, she closed her eyes and surrendered to the physical torment her mind had been denying. She sank willingly into the pit of exhaustion and pain. Her lungs ached, and her body burned in every fiber, every shrieking cell. Her muscles, joints, and bones felt damaged, battered beyond repair. But she had prevailed. . . .

Eight

Johnny watched in confusion as Honor huddled into
herself like a wounded animal. From where he sat
across the fire from her, he could see the involuntary
jerking of her muscles and nerves. He could hear
every plaintive moan. She wouldn't let him near her,
and yet she shuddered and cried out whenever a
thunderbolt exploded above them.

He didn't know what to do with her. At some point
while they'd been climbing the mountain, he'd come
to understand that she had to do this thing on her
own, but he'd never witnessed such seemingly insane determination. It made him think he didn't
know Honor Bartholomew at all.

The wind howled outside, whistling through the
cave.

She moaned, quaking with cold, and he felt a stab
of alarm. He didn't understand what she was doing,
what she was trying to prove. Was *he* the reason
she'd put herself through such hell? When he'd told
her she wouldn't make it, he hadn't meant it as a
challenge. He'd believed the mountain was too tough.
Even now he was certain it was more than his
warning that had driven her to such extremes, but
he didn't like the other option. Had her punishing

drive come out of some need to absolve herself? He knew she felt guilt about their past. He wanted her to feel guilt. But he would never have inflicted this kind of pain on her, not knowingly.

On impulse, he went to her, kneeling beside her as another spasm shook her. She was blue with cold. He touched her arm, but she cried out and fought to get away from him, thrashing like a netted bird. Her moans cut through him like a knife, and he felt a sudden and terrible need to take her into his arms, to warm her quaking body.

He moved again to touch her, and she crawled away from him, out of his reach. He backed away then, not knowing what else to do. Her terror of him paralyzed him almost as much as the powerful emotion breaking inside him. He'd never felt so helpless. All he could do was watch and wait.

Honor woke up several times during the night, once to find Johnny offering her food, which she refused. Another time, near dawn, she realized he was next to her, holding her. She wanted desperately to get away from him. She was determined to survive without his help, and she detested being the object of his pity. He paid no attention to her protests, however, and she was shaking so uncontrollably from the cold, she didn't have the energy to fight him off.

And so she surrendered, allowing him to draw her into the warmth of his embrace, allowing him to nuzzle her neck with his face as he turned her toward him and pulled her curled legs into his lap. He held her gently but firmly, enveloping her in the cocoon of his arms, his chest, and his drawn-up legs. She hated that he was treating her like an injured child, but she desperately needed the warmth of his body heat and the human contact. Her frozen limbs were beginning to respond, to sting with life as the blood resumed flowing.

She dozed off that way, enfolded in his arms and moaning with both pain and pleasure as he rubbed warmth back into her aching arms and legs. She didn't want to moan, or even to fall asleep, but she couldn't help herself. He felt good. Everything he did to her felt good, especially the way he'd coaxed her head into the curve of his neck and shoulder, then let his long black hair fall over her like a mantle.

There were times during the night when she roused and thought she must be dreaming. It didn't seem possible that it was Johnny holding her. She wouldn't have believed him capable of such kindness. Sighing, she tried to curl into him deeper, as if the heat of his body could absorb her. He seemed to sense her stirring and began to stroke her hair. Please let this be real, she prayed, appealing to the mountain spirits. Don't snatch it away from me too quickly. A tightness blocked her throat, and the empty place in her heart felt as though it was slowly being filled.

Finally she did fall into a deep, healing sleep, and it was then that the dreams actually began. At first they were womblike and nurturing, promising blissful solace. But gradually they took on another quality, softened and romantic, even sensual. They were sprinkled with images straight out of her teenage fantasies, of Johnny holding her, murmuring love words. Of her melting against him helplessly as he stroked her throat and kissed her . . .

She awoke in the morning, vaguely aware that she was stretched out facing the length of his body with one of her knees nudging his thighs and her face nuzzling into the curve of his neck. The sense of contentment she felt and the warmth of his skin were glorious. She didn't really want to wake up, or even to move, but she had the oddest, fuzziest sense that something was amiss.

Drowsily her mind began to track body parts—the top of one of his legs, the bottom of hers, the arm he'd tucked in the curve of her neck, the knee she'd pressed to his thighs. Hmmm . . . something was missing, she realized. One of her hands lay between them. The other one—

Her eyes blinked open. Where was her other hand? Gingerly she drew back and felt his muscled thighs close tightly. On her hand! She must have slipped it between his legs for warmth while she was sleeping, and now she was trapped. As she imagined the awkwardness of trying to extract it, she realized her lips were pressed wantonly to the pulse point in his throat. And worse *his* hand was draped on her hip, his fingers drifting over the rise of her fanny.

One thought, and one thought only, took possession of her mind. How was she going to get out of this situation without waking him?

She needn't have worried. Johnny's eyes were closed, but he'd been awake for a good long time— wide awake and trying to cool the fire that was roaring in his blood. His thigh muscles were rigid, and his loins throbbed with the need to roll her onto her back and find release in her soft, yielding flesh. Oh, yes, he was awake. Especially the part of him that was hard and hungry.

He could feel the nervous impulses in her trapped fingers, the involuntary tug when she'd realized her hand was caught. Every little twitch and flutter bombarded him with signals from the most erogenous of male zones. He told himself to release her, to shift his weight a little and free her hand, but his body had other ideas. It took almost as much concentrated effort to get his hormones under control as it had to climb the mountain yesterday.

Pretending to be rousing from sleep, he shifted forward as though about to roll onto his back.

Honor's soft gasp filled the cave. But instead of pulling her hand back, she panicked and jerked it upward, jamming it against his crotch.

Johnny's eyes snapped open, and his thigh muscles locked like a steel trap. "Were you looking for something?" he asked.

She stared at him, her eyes widening as she realized what she'd got a handful of. "I think I found it," she said breathlessly. Realizing her double entendre, she flushed as crimson as an Apache headband. "My hand, I mean! If you could just open your legs!"

"Oh, baby," he said softly. "You have no idea what you're asking."

Warm air rushed through her parted lips, quavering with a delicious sound. She tugged at her hand but only succeeded in getting it turned around until she was cupping him as though she'd intended to fondle him.

His thigh muscles squeezed involuntarily.

"I think I'm caught, Johnny," she said, with her marvelous knack for stating the obvious.

"I *know* you're caught." He'd been doing his damndest to keep his hands off her, but she was making that noble effort impossible. He'd told himself that after the hell she'd been through coming up the mountain, the last thing she needed was him pawing her, rolling all over her like an animal. But maybe she wanted a little pawing—maybe she wanted a lot.

"How about if you open *your* legs?" he suggested.

"My legs? Why? I mean—how would that help?"

"It would help me a lot."

Honor gazed up at him, bewildered. She could feel her whole body going weak and moist. His eyes were dark with desire, diamond-hard at the center. Still, he couldn't mean what it sounded as if he meant, could he? He'd been aroused before, but he'd always seemed to be fighting demons, fighting her. Had he just lost the battle? "I'm not sure quite what you mean. . . ."

"Sure you are," he said softly, impatiently. He feathered her cheek with his fingers, drawing them down to her mouth.

The sensation of weakness swept through her like

a warm, humid wind. "Then, you are . . . talking about sex? About making love? To me?"

"Don't make it sound so complicated. Men and women have been doing it for ages." His voice had the raw, sexy edge of a man pushed beyond his limits. "Don't tell me you've never fantasized about us doing that?"

Yes, she'd fantasized about it. Last night, and countless other nights since he'd disappeared from her life. She'd had dreams of him seducing her slowly, drugging her with desire as only he could. She had dreamed of him kissing her until she was insensate with passion, dreamed of him taking her with his dark animal hunger. She had dreamed so vividly, she knew it wasn't safe to answer his question.

When she didn't, he captured her chin and drew her head up, stroking her throat with his thumb. "So tell me, Honor. Do you want me to do that to you? Say it, baby. Would you like to feel me inside you?"

Honor's stomach clutched with shock as much as excitement. His voice was rough around the edges. His eyes were black with passion, but there were flashes of another emotion electrifying their depths. The impulses registered on her every nerve ending. He was angry, she realized. Even if he wasn't consciously aware of it, the darkness was there, triggered by the heat of his passion, feeding his desire. Damn him, she thought, her throat aching. She knew she ought to back away, but she couldn't. The raw, sexy edge of his anger thrilled her.

"Yes," she said, her voice gravelly, "I want you inside me."

Johnny exhaled, heat pouring through his nostrils. He stared at her for one long, hot moment, on the brink of something reckless. His body throbbed; his mind shouted out an executive command that he act. God knew he wanted her. He'd always wanted her. She was the girl of his teenage dreams—and she was telling him *yes, I want you inside me.*

His heart was beating as wildly as it had when he first met her. His stomach was as painfully knotted with aching desire. Pain, he thought. This wasn't pleasure, it was pain. He was as crazy as that idiot kid had been, as racked with need and out of control. But that kid had wanted only one thing—to win her love, to worship at her feet. The grown man had other dangerous impulses. He wouldn't stop at winning her love. He wanted revenge.

He shifted his weight and felt her hand slip away from the heat between his thighs. She'd escaped him. His reaction was swift and angry. Burying his hand in her lush hair, he pulled her toward him and lifted her mouth to his.

Her lips parted in trembling surrender. She whimpered, the sound rife with uncertainty and desire.

That sound thrilled him.

"Johnny," she implored, "love me . . . don't hurt me."

"Love you," he breathed, his mouth on hers. His stomach muscles clenched. That was all he wanted, wasn't it? In the deepest part of his soul? Just to love her? Still to love her?

He let his mouth linger over hers interminably, prolonging the agony. He ached to kiss her, to ravish her mouth, to thrust his tongue deep into the tender channel of her throat. He ached to invade every part of her, every orifice. He wanted to take carnal possession, to mark her and make her his. But once he let go of that last thread of restraint, once the cage door was open . . .

Gradually he became aware of the anguish in her breathing and opened his eyes. He saw pain in the set of her mouth, the sweet suffering in her gaze, and he drew back, confused. It took him only a moment to realize what had happened. *He was hurting her.* The hand he'd buried in her braid was clenched, gripping her hair tightly. His other hand had closed on her forearm, compressing the cuts and bruises.

The sight of her brought as vivid a flash of understanding as if he'd had one of his grandfather's dreams. "I can't love you, Honor," he said with a hard, despairing sigh. "Not without hurting you. It's impossible."

He released her and rolled away, sitting up, his shoulders hunched forward, his legs drawn up. His loins were still pumping with heat and blood.

"Johnny?" Her voice was soft, shaking. "I'm all right, really. I'm not hurt, if that's what you're thinking."

But you will be. Count on it.

She touched his shoulder, and he shook his head. "Don't be a fool, Honor. You've been done a favor."

He rose to his feet and walked to the mouth of the cave. He'd just had the perfect opportunity to take his revenge, but he hadn't done it. The thought of hurting her had appalled him. The impulse inside him had been to save her, to protect her. He couldn't seem to get near the woman without turning into a white knight.

The thunderstorm had passed, he realized, looking around at the craggy peaks of the mountain range. The day was bright and sunny, rainwashed. He only wished the storm inside him could dissipate as quickly and leave such beauty behind.

Narrowing his eyes against the sharpness of the sunlight, he walked out into the warm blue sky and let the light bathe him, soothe him. He wanted that connection with the elements now. In his childhood nature had been his only respite, the only thing that could heal him. It had offered him a serenity that nothing else could.

A short time later he heard Honor move around behind him. He turned to find her brushing hair out of her eyes and blinking against the brightness. In the torn camp dress and with her blond tresses flying free of the braid that hung down her back, she looked like a wild mountain woman.

It was a sight he'd never expected to see, and it had an odd effect on him. It liberated his mind for an instant. The girl called Honor was imperfect and real, he realized. She was flesh and blood, not the fantasized ideal he'd held in his mind for eighteen years. The insight made him want to lift her in his arms and swing her around, celebrating the morning, the sunlight.

"I wish you could see yourself now," he said, his voice growing husky as he remembered how he'd cradled her in his arms the night before. "I don't know how to describe it. You're earthy. You're beautiful."

"Don't do that!" She turned on him furiously. "I won't allow you to shove me away and then turn around and tell me I'm beautiful . . . and *earthy*."

He shrugged an apology, genuinely surprised. Somehow he'd missed a note in his analysis of the new Honor. She was angry. Spitfire angry. She drove home that fact as she whirled around and started down the mountain. He could hardly blame her. He wanted her one minute, hated himself for wanting her the next. He was at war, and she was getting caught in the cross fire.

He could see her limping and knew she must be in considerable pain. His own muscles were as tender as bruises from yesterday's climb. Hers must have been torn apart by it. He'd seen the cuts on her arms and legs, but it was also clear that she wasn't in any mood to accept aid and comfort.

She stumbled and caught herself, swearing so loudly even he could hear it. He decided to hang back and give her plenty of room. There was nothing to be gained in crowding an angry woman. But he smiled when she faltered again, then picked up a loose rock and flung it out of her way. The amusement he felt had an odd quality of sympathy to it, sympathy that for once wasn't driven by guilt or tainted with anger.

His ancestors would have called it softening toward the enemy, he realized. And there was no greater shame for an Apache warrior. A man's honor, his very life, depended on his ability to deal swiftly and mercilessly with anyone who threatened his survival, or the survival of his tribe. It was a violent code for a violent existence.

She did qualify as a threat, he reminded himself, watching her disappear down the trail. He'd been emotionally mugged by that sweet thing in blue chintz and braided hair. She had ripped his heart out when he'd been young and stupid, and if he hadn't learned anything from that experience, then he deserved whatever he got.

Still, he though, watching her yellow hair swing in the sunlight, she was changing, transforming before his very eyes into a female even more irresistible than the one he remembered. Fortunately she was angrier than hell at the moment and wouldn't let him near her. If he thought he'd done her a favor by backing off in the cave, he knew with the utmost certainty that she was doing him a favor by being furious with him now.

He drew a deep breath and started down the mountain after her. They were about to spend several more days together alone in these mountains. He didn't want to think about what would happen if they both let their guard down at once.

"The moon! Look, there's a ring around it," Honor said, pointing up at the night sky. A silvery nimbus surrounded a moon so full it seemed about to give birth.

Johnny twisted to look up where Honor was pointing. The campfire they sat at had burned down low, making it easy to see even the tiniest stars sparkling above them.

"It's beautiful, isn't it?" she said, turning back to Johnny's mysterious smile. "And very mystical," she added. "Does it mean something?"

He just shrugged, which piqued her curiosity.

After the climb that morning, and out of necessity, they'd spent most of the rest of the day gathering food. It had been a tense but bearable experience once she'd decided it was pointless being angry at someone as unpredictable as Johnny. Tonight, after a meal of roasted rabbit, mescal, and acorns, they'd both relaxed a little.

"Is that a smile?" she persisted, searching his darkly handsome face. "What's going on? Does it mean something spooky? Like zombies rising from their graves?"

"Not even close. I don't know if there's any official meaning, but when I was a kid and the moon got like that, I used to hear the women whispering about 'love magic.'"

"What's love magic?"

"Remember, you asked."

She laughed. "I'm holding my breath here."

"It's a spell used to attract lovers. In its strongest form, *godistso nca*, it creates an uncontrollable obsession to be with the one who cast the spell."

"Sounds romantic."

He sat forward, long hair flowing around him as he regarded the fire. "That depends on your point of view," he said finally, looking up at her. "The obsession is sexual. The object of the spell becomes a love slave."

"Love slave?" Honor fingered the long rip in the neckline of her blouse. The tears in her blouse and skirt had happened yesterday on her trip up the mountain, but now she felt as if her clothes were falling off. "And how do you— I mean, how does one cast such a spell?"

He shrugged again, his smile faintly wicked. The fire painted the bronzed angles of his face with liquid gold. "I never got into sorcery."

Her whistle of relief seemed to intrigue him, and she found herself wishing she could look away from the golden flames reflected in his eyes. He didn't need sorcery. All he had to do was catch a woman in his gaze, in the luminous glare of his panther eyes, and she was helplessly ensnared—his quivering prey, his love slave, or whatever his mercurial mood dictated.

Almost involuntarily Honor glanced over at the lean-to, his "bedroom" out-of-doors. Was she going to be sleeping in there with him? That didn't seem a wise idea given their track record.

"We'll do it back-to-back," he said.

"What?"

"Sleep. Tonight. Back-to-back shouldn't get us in too much trouble."

"As long as we stay that way."

Her words were prophetic. They fell asleep back-to-back, but woke up face-to-face, her leg thrown over his hip, the back of her hand pressed into his pelvis.

"Do you think you could find another place for that?" he asked, indicating her hand.

He was surprisingly polite, considering everything.

"It must have been the moon," Honor explained.

That day he showed her how the Apache hunted waterfowl without weapons. He floated gourds in a pond full of ducks until the ducks accepted the objects drifting among them. Then he made himself a gourd mask and entered the pool, submerging until only the gourd showed. Within seconds he was close enough to a duck to touch it. He was about to grab its little webbed feet and pull it under when Honor realized what he was going to do and let out a shriek.

"Don't drown that duck!" she cried.

"You would have been one hungry Indian," Johnny told her as waterfowl scattered far and wide.

That night they feasted on nuts, seeds, and berries and gazed uneasily at the ringed moon. The next morning it was Johnny who had his hand in the wrong place when they woke up. He was curled behind her, cupping her breast. He released her immediately, but it was too late to do Honor any good. She had already melted like a quart of ice cream left out at a birthday party. His touch enthralled her, showering her with hot jets of pleasure. Her dreams paled in comparison to the real thing. "It was your turn," she assured him earnestly, hoping to give him a hint.

Johnny didn't need hints. He already had the combined sex drive of ten rutting stags. The way she'd caressed him the night before with her white-hot fingertips, it was a miracle all he did was touch her. He wanted to shake her naked body with his deep thrusts. He wanted to feel her clutching at him, to hear her throaty screams of pleasure.

He'd been aroused for days on end without relief. It wouldn't have surprised him if this was another part of the test his grandfather had in mind. Warrior training, he thought, smiling grimly. Get a man as hard as a war club and keep him that way day and night. It was guaranteed to put him in a fighting mood.

But as the days wore on, it was her ability to endure hardship that most challenged his assumptions about her. Strength and bravery weren't qualities he'd expected from her, but she didn't shrink from the creatures that howled by night or the grueling excursions to find food during the day. She was generous to a fault, sharing whatever she'd foraged with him, even when there was barely enough for her. She wasn't acting like the kind of woman who would betray a man lightly, he admitted to himself.

An uneasy bond formed between them. Johnny told himself it was an alliance against the elements. They had to cooperate to survive. He even found a way to reduce the agony of their sleeping arrangements. He would wait until she was asleep before joining her in the lean-to.

On this particular night he waited even longer than usual, but Honor was still awake when he entered. She was holding something in her hand when she glanced up and saw him. Quickly she slipped it into the pocket of her dress.

"What are you doing?" Johnny asked. He'd got a glimpse of what looked like a small blue stone, similar to one of the charms in his medicine bag.

"Nothing, really. A good-luck piece I brought with me."

Her vague smile made him suspicious. Still, he couldn't imagine that she would have gone through his medicine bag. "What is it, Honor?"

"Nothing," she said, a note of urgency in her voice. "Let it go, okay?"

Distrust was seeping into his blood, threatening the tentative bond that was developing between them. "Honor, don't do this," he said softly. "Talk to me. We have a bargain, remember? You agreed to do whatever I asked."

She shook her head and rolled away from him, assuming the position she slept in. "I don't care what I agreed to," she said. "It's late, and I'm tired."

He put a hand on her shoulder, and she jerked away from him. "Johnny, don't!"

Sensing the depth of her turmoil, he backed off.

Gradually she turned to face him, and with great reluctance drew the stone from her pocket. Johnny struggled to breathe as he stared at the triangular piece of turquoise, one of the strongest of the Apache medicine charms.

"You gave it to me," she said, "a long time ago."

"I know." He had given her the charm before going

to trial on the assault-and-battery charges. He'd had no idea then how things would turn out, that she would testify against him. But perhaps he'd had a premonition that he might never see her again.

She sat up and brought the stone to her mouth, pressing it against the softness of her lower lip, unaware of how penitent the gesture looked. Finally, with great difficulty, she spoke. "'No matter what happens, Honor, keep this. Remember me.'"

She looked up at him, tears sparkling in her eyes. "That's what you said to me."

The pain Johnny felt was so razor-sharp, he had to suck in air to control it. He turned away from her, his eyes unfocused, his mind riveted on the past. He remembered the words, and every ragged breath he'd had to take to find the control to say them.

"I kept it," she whispered. "I didn't forget."

"Honor, don't—" Even her voice stabbed at him. He couldn't let her resurrect that memory. It was the pocket where all his pain resided. He couldn't even let her express her anguish about that day, because it touched his own. He would never forget the awkwardness, the naked misery, with which he tried to say "Remember me" and ended up saying good-bye. His sixteen-year-old heart had felt as though it were bursting.

"Johnny, please . . . ? Can we talk?"

"No," he said harshly. In her desperation to make things right, she kept blundering into his wounds. "You said you were tired. Get some sleep."

He heard her sink down on the bed of leaves that made up the floor of the lean-to. Rigid with the need to gain control of his emotions, he sat with his back to her. He couldn't move. He felt as if he'd been opened up and gutted, but left alive. If he thrashed like a mortally wounded animal, if he tried to get away, he might bleed to death.

It seemed that hours had passed before he finally lay down, his back to hers, bare skin against blue

chintz. Rigidly still, he was aware of the movement of
her shoulders against his as she breathed. He could
feel the place where her lower back sloped away from
his and then returned in the yielding warmth of her
buttocks. The experience of his own grief had height-
ened all his senses. He was as exquisitely tuned in to
her as if their nervous systems were linked at the
places where their spines touched. He could hear the
shallow rasp of her breath, and he knew somehow
that she was trying not to cry. He could feel her
hopelessness, her sadness.

Honor, he thought, what happened?

She shifted, and he felt her moving, turning toward him.

His heart pounding, he waited until she was facing
his back. And then he turned too.

If there was any resistance left in him at all, it was
gone the instant he caught a glimpse of her beautiful, tear-streaked face. He dragged her into his arms.

"Johnny—"

"Hush," he said, "hush." Pain ripped a piece from
his heart as he clutched her close. The torment he'd
been fighting for so long, for years, poured over the
wound like a river of fire. It was the fiercest, sweetest
agony he'd ever known. Vaguely aware that he was
crushing her in his arms, and that he didn't want to
hurt her, he understood only that he had to survive
the assault somehow. He couldn't let her speak, not
even to comfort him. He couldn't let her do anything
that might unleash the horrible wonder of what was
happening inside him.

Finally he released her, and she buried her face in
his hair and heaved a trembling sigh. They held each
other that way for a long time, enemies of the heart
thrown together by some mysterious design, brought
to their knees by the truth of their shared humanity.

"Johnny," she whispered, "is it all right between
us now?"

He knew what she was asking, and he had so

many reasons not to answer her. It was a dangerous question, badly timed. But he was vulnerable now, opened, and he couldn't resist it. Feelings were flowing that he'd held in check for so long. There were things he didn't understand. Questions that needed answers.

He drew back from her, deliberating. Her grave blue eyes and tear-streaked smile broke his heart.

"What is it?" she asked.

He followed the path of her tears with his forefinger, surprised at his own need to be tender. "Why didn't you tell me you were going to testify?" he asked. "Even if you believed you were doing the right thing, why didn't you warn me? We were friends, Honor. Friends watch out for each other; they protect each other."

"They told me I couldn't talk to you, Johnny, not once I'd agreed to be a witness for the prosecution. My father said there would be a mistrial—"

"Your father hated me. How could you have believed anything he said?"

Tears glittered. "I had to, Johnny. I didn't know what else to do!"

He stared down at her, regret flaring through him. Why was he doing this? Why was he putting her to a test he knew she couldn't pass? The bond he'd felt went beyond friendship. He would have done anything for her, sacrificed his life. And yet she'd been afraid to stand up to her father. God, it destroyed him to think that she hadn't even found a way to warn him.

"Johnny, please. I was frightened for you!"

"Frightened for me? When the prosecutor asked you if I had violent tendencies, you told him yes. When he asked if I'd threatened to kill those boys, you said yes—" He broke off as the pain resurged.

"But, Johnny, what else could I do? What else could I say? I couldn't lie on the witness stand."

Her desperation was heartbreaking. It tugged at

him, but he couldn't let himself respond. There was too much misery, too much grief. He was already shutting down, he realized, moving away from her emotionally. His heart was growing cold again, and there was nothing he could do to stop it. He could almost forgive her the testimony because she'd been tricked. But whether it came out of his Apache heritage or out of the terrible isolation of his childhood, he couldn't forgive her for not being the friend he'd needed, the friend he would have been to her.

"I can't stay here tonight," he said.

"Why? Where are you going?"

"I don't know—anywhere but here." He pushed to his feet, brushing the leaves from his legs. His food pouch and knife were by the campfire. As he started to get them, she came out of the lean-to and called his name. He didn't stop.

"Johnny, I won't let you do this to me again! If you go, I'll—"

She was shaking with anger. He could hear it in her voice.

"You'll what?" he said, turning to her.

She dragged in a breath, as though preparing to blast him. Instead she shrugged helplessly. "I don't know . . . just don't do it." Tears welled in her eyes. "Don't go."

Johnny breathed a harsh word, but it wasn't anger burning inside him now; it was sadness. His heart was a fiery hole in his chest as he turned and walked away from her, into the dark soul of the forest.

Nine

Honor woke up half-frozen and barely able to uncoil
from the ball she'd curled into. Her first awareness
was of the warm spot on her back, apparently from a
ray of sunshine poking through a hole in the lean-to
roof. Her second awareness was that she had spent
the night alone. Johnny hadn't come back, she
realized, as she glanced out at the dead ashes of the
campfire.

She quickly gathered kindling and got the fire
going again, huddling next to it until she was warm
enough to consider her next most pressing concern,
hunger. Johnny had dug a pit and lined it with rocks
to store the food they foraged. Her mouth actually
watered at the thought of a meal of nuts, seeds, and
unripe berries.

Once she'd eaten, and the day loomed ahead, she
dealt with her third concern, Johnny. It rather pleased
her that he'd come in a poor third among her prior-
ities. Beyond the simmering hurt and anger she felt,
it gave her hope that she might be getting her
emotional house in order where he was concerned. If
there was anything more she could have done to gain
his understanding and forgiveness, she didn't know
what it was. She couldn't change what had hap-

pened, and she was beginning to think that enduring eighteen years of guilt was enough atonement for any sinner, no matter what the poor wretch had done.

She busied herself with gathering fresh bedding for the lean-to and with replenishing their food stores, but as the morning wore on and Johnny didn't return, she couldn't deny that she was worried. She told herself that her concerns about him were pointless, that he'd probably gone back up the mountain to the cave. He was a big boy, after all, and he had survived several days alone before she arrived.

As she packed the last of the supplies she'd gathered into the pit, she became aware of the grime caked on her arms. She scrubbed away at it with her fingers, knowing it was hopeless. She was as ripe as a bag lady, covered with pungent layers of sweat and Mother Nature's plenitude. Even her hair was matted and tangled with leaves and twigs. She needed a bath, a shampoo. "A manicure," she murmured, smiling at how absurd a prospect that was.

The river where Johnny had found her was the nearest source of fresh water, and she and Johnny had traveled back to it several times to fill the small barrel he'd made from the bark of a birch tree. Now the thought of all that fresh running water on her hot, sweat-coated skin was enough to make her shiver with anticipation.

A short time later she stood on the river's turbulent banks, watching the churning white water and savoring the shade of the trees that bordered its shores. The rich scent of pine pierced her senses. The river was exhilarating and calming at the same time, she realized, exactly the sort of place where a soiled woman could cleanse body and spirit. Perhaps that sense of redemption and renewal was what she'd always loved about rushing water, even the stream where she and Johnny used to meet.

Once she'd found a calm spot in the turbulence, she knelt on the river's rocky shore to crush the aloe root she'd brought with her. Johnny had told her how to work the pulp into a foamy froth that would serve as soap.

Moments later, naked as the day she came into the world, she crouched calf-deep in the icy mountain stream, washing out her camp dress and her underwear. When she was done, she laid the clothing out on the rocks to dry. Finally, freeing her braided hair—and her modest soul—she waded into the river and dived.

The water was bracingly cold and heavenly wet, the answer to her dreams. Once the shock of its icy temperature had worn off, Honor swam and cavorted with a freedom she hadn't felt since childhood, and perhaps not even then. The pressure of the water surging against her skin felt delicious, as did the bubbles that churned from the turbulence upstream.

She dived deep and resurfaced again and again, letting the water stream over her body and flinging her head back to toss her hair off her face. Being naked was wonderful, liberating, and Honor was delighted at her own lack of inhibitions. Refreshed, she finally waded toward shore to get the aloe root and wash herself.

Standing thigh-deep in the swirling currents, she soaped down her shoulders and arms with great satisfaction. She was getting ready to wash her hair when her pulse quickened in response to something she sensed more than heard. Above the rush of the water, a crackling sound caught her attention. She glanced up, scanning the trees, and spotted a sight that paralyzed her.

A man was watching her, standing in the shadows.

She couldn't make out his features because of the light at his back, but she recognized his broad shoulders and his long hair. It must be Johnny, she realized. He'd been watching her bathe. Honor resisted the impulse to dive in the water and escape his eyes. Something held her there, barely breathing.

She was sharply aware of her own nakedness, and of the effect it might have on him. She knew he must have fantasized about her; she had about him often enough. But she'd never imagined him watching her this way. Did she look the way he'd expected? She'd always thought of herself as too thin and pale. The kids had teased her about being all bones in high school. Did Johnny find her pretty? A desirable woman?

All of those questions rushed through her mind as she glanced down at her own body and saw the beads of moisture clinging to her skin. Her breasts were full and flushed with color, perhaps from the invigorating swim. Whatever the reason, they looked larger than she remembered, and heavier. Her nipples were hardened and tingling.

She felt a stirring of excitement as she surveyed her own jutting hipbones and the golden delta of hair that crowned her womanhood. The rise and fall of her belly as she breathed made her realize how sleek and sensual a woman's body could look when sheened with water. She was seeing herself through a man's eyes, through his eyes.

She began to wash herself, drawing the foamy material across the rise of her chest. Bubbles streamed over her breasts and down her torso, clinging to the sensitive crests of her nipples and hiding in the crevice of her belly button. Her stomach muscles tightened as she imagined his finger tracing the same path.

A shudder went through her that was as deep and sexual as anything she'd ever felt. Stimulation showered her senses. She was breathing deeply, heatedly. She wanted him, his touch. Johnny—

A cracking sound exploded in her head. It sounded like a gunshot, but as her eyes flew open, she knew it must have been a twig snapping under someone's foot. A man stood on the bank before her, as plain as day, but it took Honor several stunned seconds to come to grips with what she was seeing. He *wasn't* Johnny.

He was tall, even taller than Johnny, with storm-blown blond hair that swept back from his face and cascaded down his back. His brawny build and the black bandanna he wore tied around his head might have marked him as a biker if it hadn't been for his marine fatigues. The olive-drab T-shirt and flak vest made him look like a soldier of fortune.

"Who are you?" she breathed. Without waiting for the man to answer, she turned and plunged into the river.

"Where is she?" Johnny was both angry and alarmed as he searched the empty campsite, looking for Honor. He'd returned, planning to break camp and head back to Whiteriver, and much as he might have wanted to, he couldn't leave her behind in the mountains.

He hadn't completed all the tests required of him, but he'd had all he could handle of waiting for the spirits to speak and sleeping in a lean-to with a woman he wanted but was afraid to touch. He assumed she felt the same way. Now where the hell was she?

After a quick search of the surrounding woods with no sign of Honor, Johnny returned to the campsite. He'd just set about dismantling the lean-to when he heard someone—or something—crashing through the trees toward the camp. He couldn't imagine anything but a large animal making that much noise? A bear? Drawing the knife from his moccasin, he slipped behind the cover of the lean-to.

"Starhawk?"

The male voice sounded familiar, but Johnny watched and waited until the intruder came into view. He recognized the wild blond hair and black bandanna first. Johnny swore softly and rose from his hiding place as his former partner strode into the campsite. "Dias!" he growled in disbelief. "What are you doing here?"

Geoff Dias took one look at Johnny's loincloth and roared with laughter. "They told me you were on some kind of quest, but I didn't believe them. I had to check it out for myself! What are you doing, buddy? Playing cowboys and Indians?"

"That's right." With a movement so swift it was barely discernible, Johnny sent his knife whistling past Geoff's blond mane and stuck it in the snow-white back of an aspen tree just behind him. "And I'm damn good at it too."

Geoff glanced over his shoulder at the quivering knife handle. "Hey! Only kidding."

Johnny nodded and grinned. "Right, me too."

A moment later the two men, one dark as a jungle panther, the other tawny and golden as a mountain lion, were hugging and cuffing each other on the back.

"What are you doing here?" Johnny asked, pushing his old friend away good-naturedly.

Geoff chuckled, a wicked gleam in his rich green eyes. "You won't believe me if I tell you. There's some naked honey taking a bath down by the river."

"A woman?"

"Yeah." Geoff's expression said what else? "She's gorgeous, man, and hotter than the pistons on my Harley."

Johnny had a bad feeling about Geoff's little adventure at the river. A very bad feeling. "What did she look like?" he asked.

"A beauty. Long blond hair, long neck. Slim, but built—you know." He cupped imaginary breasts and laughed, a husky male sound. "She looked right at me, man."

"She saw you?" Johnny's hands curled into fists. *"She knew you were watching her?"*

"Hell, yes, she saw me. I thought she was going to ask me to scrub her back."

By this time Johnny knew he had to be talking about Honor. How many women could there be on this mountain who fit that description? As Geoff went on, describing Honor's body in detail, Johnny saw red. Blood red. For all of the emotion and heat and turmoil that he and Honor had been through, Johnny had never seen her naked, and he couldn't stand the thought that Geoff Dias had. He could easily have killed his long-lost buddy. At the very least he wanted to rearrange his handsome face.

"Bastard," Johnny muttered.

"What's the problem?"

"You're the problem!" Johnny snagged Geoff's vest, jerked him forward, and launched a fist toward his chin. The blow that connected was an uppercut that should have knocked Geoff's head off. When it didn't, Johnny backed it up with a powerful left hook. The one-two punch set Geoff on his butt.

Geoff shook his head like a stunned prizefighter. "What's going on?" he said, glaring up at Johnny as he worked his jaw. "You got me all the way up here to fight?"

Johnny had no idea what he was talking about. "What do you mean, *I* got you up here? What are you doing here?"

"I got a call from a friend of yours. She said she was calling from the reservation, and you needed some surveillance done on a uranium-mining operation. When I showed up at Whiteriver, they told me you were up here."

Johnny was already regretting his decision to contact Geoff. He should have known better. Dias couldn't be trusted around anything that shaved its legs, much less a beautiful woman. Since their glory days together rescuing POWs and hostages for the

Pentagon, Geoff had become the "bad boy" of the American press. The fact that he was still doing recovery work on a mercenary-for-hire basis added to his roughneck glamour. Women couldn't seem to resist the man's raffish smile, and if that didn't get them, the sexy, come-get-it-baby rumble of his motorcycle did.

Still, the fact that Honor had contacted Geoff didn't explain what he was doing up here in the mountains, skulking around like a Peeping Tom. "That operation's in the hills near Coyote Gulch. Did you get lost trying to find it?"

"I'm way ahead of you, Starhawk. I've already been to the site, and I've got all the evidence you'll ever need."

Johnny rubbed his fist. He was still furious, but Geoff's claim had piqued his curiosity. "Documented evidence?"

"A photo album—you'll love it. I've got copies of one of their own 'confidential' environmental impact studies, which shows the seepage from their holding pond is polluting the groundwater."

That might have been good news to Johnny under other circumstances, but he wasn't in the mood to congratulate his ex-partner at the moment, or to explain why he'd tried to knock his teeth out. "How'd you get up here?" he asked.

"Rode my bike until the trail gave out, then I hiked the rest of the way." His dark gold eyebrows lifted innocently. "Did I come at a bad time? Woman trouble?"

"You could say that." Johnny's cold laughter was meant to be anything but humorous. "Go back down and wait for me at the tribal headquarters in Whiteriver. I'll be back tonight or tomorrow at the latest. We'll talk then."

"No problem," Geoff said, more than happy to end the hostilities. He pushed to his feet and brushed the dust from his jeans. Geoff Dias liked a good fight as well as the next guy. He was at least an inch taller than Johnny and probably outweighed him by fifteen pounds. But he'd known Johnny for a dozen years, ever since their days in the marines, and he knew what the half-breed Apache was capable of. Whatever had ticked his friend off this time, Johnny wasn't just angry—he was in a murderous rage.

Honor knew something was terribly wrong the moment she got a glimpse of the campsite. The roof of the lean-to had been demolished, and the coals from the fire were strewn everywhere. She called out Johnny's name, half-afraid that the stranger who'd been watching her at the river would appear. Or that he'd already been there. Was he the one who'd destroyed their camp?

"How was your swim?"

The harsh question seemed to come from out of nowhere. Honor turned to see Johnny walking toward her from the gloom of the pine forest. She was instantly aware of the smoldering anger he carried with him like a shroud. "How did you know I was swimming?" she asked.

"Your friend told me."

His voice was low, dangerously controlled. Honor wet her lips, sensing the kind of latent violence that would force such control. "He wasn't my friend," she said quickly. "I never saw him before. Do you know him?"

"That doesn't matter now. I want to know why you did it."

"Did what?"

"Performed for him."

"I didn't perform for him! How could you think that?"

Hellfire leaped in Johnny's dark eyes. "You knew he was there. You looked right at him."

"I couldn't see him in the light. I knew *someone*

was there, that's all. I didn't know who he was. He had long hair. I thought—" She broke off, realizing what she was about to say.

"You thought what?" Johnny went still, as taut and alert as a big cat who'd caught the scent of his prey. "You thought *what*? That it was me?"

She flushed hotly and looked away.

Johnny's heart was pounding thunderously. All he could see was the disarray of her still-wet hair, and the way her damp dress clung to her body. He couldn't bear the thought of another man seeing her naked, lusting after her. But that didn't drive him as wild as the possibility that she might have liked having another man's eyes on her.

"Honor . . . did you think it was me watching you?"

With a sharp cry of defiance she met his eyes. "Do you wish it had been you watching me? Instead of him?"

Jealousy ignited Johnny's rage. Insanity reigned. He'd never wanted to manhandle a woman before, but that impulse was exploding through him now. He reached out, his hand shaking, and clenched his fist in the air. *Yes, he wished it had been him, God, how he wished it had been him!*

"Get your clothes off," he said, barely able to get the words out.

"What?"

"You heard me. Strip down—the way you were at the river when you thought someone was watching."

She stepped back, fear rising in her eyes.

But Johnny didn't give a damn about her fear. He didn't give a damn about anything but making her pay for the agony she was putting him through. The only thing that mattered to him now was personal pain, and personal justice. She could rip him apart with a word, a look. Now it was his turn to do some ripping, even if it was just her clothes.

She turned as if to bolt, and he stopped her escape with one lunging step. "Show me what you showed him," he said, burying his hand in her damp hair and pulling her to him. She went rigid in his arms, but her breasts were soft against his rib cage. Her heart was pounding like that of a wild animal.

"Do it," he said. "You performed for him. Now perform for me!"

Honor choked back a cry of outrage. "No, I won't!" She knew he was furious enough to hurt her, but she'd taken all the abuse she could tolerate. She couldn't do what he asked. "Let go of me!"

"Not until you're naked."

He reached for the neckline of her blouse, and Honor twisted away, thrashing at him, screaming as his hand closed on the loose material. She reared back, and the placket of her blouse ripped out, buttons flying.

"Let me go!" she cried, her fingernails raking down his arm. A soft gasp filled her throat when she saw what she'd done.

Johnny grimaced in pain as he stared at the nasty crimson slash on his forearm. "You've drawn blood," he said. "Again."

She tried to wrench away from him, a sob in her throat as he caught her by the wrist, locking her still.

"Bastard!" She whirled on him, glaring at him furiously.

Their eyes clashed and held, full of heat and fight and fury. The air came alive with their hot, panting breaths. Honor moaned, blinking away tears, refusing to expose any more of the hurt and anger she felt to his eyes. She would not cry. She would strangle on her own tears before she let that happen!

Johnny tightened his grip, exerting a pressure that forced her closer. He loathed his own lack of control, but emotion was battering him like a hailstorm. He wanted her with a passion that was blinding. And he resented her with that same staggering passion. That was what he couldn't forgive, he realized. She had made him feel again. He hated her because he *did* feel something for her—something beautiful and terrible—even though he was desperate not to feel anything!

He caught her by the arms, fury locked in his rigid muscles. The sight of her flying hair and flashing eyes aroused him to a fever pitch of pain and desire. "Bitch," he whispered, the word shaking on his breath, as he lifted her to his mouth and kissed her.

Honor stiffened against him for an instant, and then her body went limp. The touch of his lips sapped her of all strength. It dragged her under like the river. She couldn't fight him any longer. If he was so determined to punish her for the past, then let him do it. She just wanted it over with. The panther had caught his prey. Now let him tear it apart, limb from limb, devour it.

"I hate you," Johnny breathed against her mouth. The emotion was raw, true. It came straight from his clenched gut. But his tone was hushed and reverent, and another word was locked in his heart, a word that was threatening to claw through his rib cage from the inside, to split open his chest.

Love. He still loved her.

The realization confounded him. It rocked him with wonder and despair. He didn't want to let himself believe it, but the force of it overwhelmed him, pounding at him until he had no choice. He held her back, staring at her tear-streaked face and wild hair. "Honor?" he groaned, dragging her into his arms. "Honor, what is this? What are we doing to each other?"

"Johnny," she sobbed out, "I'm sorry."

Her broken cries came at him like physical blows. They knocked the sense out of him. He held her tightly, crushing her to him, his defenses destroyed. He didn't know what to do anymore. He didn't know how to stop the chaos. He had to be with her. He had to make love to her. There was no longer a choice. It had all caught up with him, all the wild longing, the desire to connect, the brutal need to love her, to hurt her.

He swung an arm under her legs and picked her up, carrying her over to the remains of the lean-to. But as he knelt to settle her on the leafy bed, she clung to him tightly, forcing him to reach behind his neck in order to disengage her hands. "Honor?"

Her hands clenched into fists, and he was struck by the torment in her beautiful gray eyes. "You want this, don't you?" he asked.

"Y-yes," she said, "it's all I've ever wanted."

Johnny's gut twisted with understanding. There was anguish in getting what you've always dreamed of yet never thought you'd have. He felt it too. He was so hard for her now, so urgently in need of her soft depths, it was dangerous even to touch her. He looked down at her, taking in her pale beauty, hardly able to believe what he was about to do to her, the woman he couldn't even touch all those years ago.

Honor tried to unclench her hands and couldn't. Her stomach muscles went rigid with anticipation as he began to undress her, gently peeling away the damp clothing. His hands were shaking against her flesh, and he dragged in a hard, shuddering breath when she was finally naked.

His gaze prowled her exposed body so intimately, it made her ache and swell with desire. Deep inside she felt as though she were being crowded and squeezed, like a ruffle of heavy satin being drawn unbearably tight. She could almost feel him touching her as he ran his hungry gaze over her breasts, caressing her nipples and bringing them to tingling points of pleasure.

She arched uncontrollably, waiting for his hands, but he seemed determined to hold himself back. Even his breathing slowed, becoming heated and sensual as he visually stroked her belly and feathered her inner thighs. The sensations he elicited were unbearable. They demanded release, relief! But all she could do was lie there, letting him ravish her with his eyes.

Johnny was aroused by every facet of her nakedness, the swollen softness of her breasts, the quiver of her taut stomach muscles. It still enraged him to think that Geoff Dias had seen her this way, that any man ever had or ever might see her this way. A terrible need to possess her burned through his muscles, but he fought it into submission, forcing himself to be gentle as he flattened his hand on her naked belly.

"Johnny?" she asked thickly. "What is it?" Her gray eyes were smoky with desire, misted with concern.

He captured her gaze and held it, willing her not to look away from him. "The thought of another man seeing you like this drives me wild," he said, splaying his fingers wide as though to lay claim to her being. Gentle, he told himself. Don't hurt her, you bastard.

"Johnny, *please*," she said. "I thought he was you. I wanted him to be you, only you!"

"I can't help it." He slid his hand up to her breast and cupped her possessively. "I can't stand the thought of any other man doing this to you, touching you this way."

A whimper caught in her throat, and the sweet sound of it drove him crazy with desire. His fingers contracted on her breast, and all the gentleness went out of him. "This is mine," he said, his voice breaking. "This part of you, every part of you, inside and out, mine."

Honor lost control under the rough beauty of his hands. Tears broke, scalding tears. Her response to his passion was utter, shuddering helplessness. A cry of need flared from somewhere inside her.

He bent to kiss her, and she arched against his hand, astonished by the sexual longing that shot through her. His mouth was hot and urgent. His touch was possessive, yet incredibly tender. Every slow flex of his fingers seemed to feed into the nerves that ran straight to the core of her.

He slid an arm beneath her shoulder and lifted her, nuzzling her hair, murmuring his need for her and all the things he wanted to do to her. He melted her with his husky, sensual whispered secrets in her ear. He promised the forbidden. And then his long fingers began to stroke those places where his gaze had been, her belly, her thighs, and she dissolved into a hot jet stream of wanting him.

She gasped softly, bewildered as he released her and rolled to a sitting position, stripping off his breechcloth and moccasins. But a moment later he was looming over her again, and the power of his body was enthralling. His shoulders rippled with muscle as he braced himself above her. His eyes flashed with a pantherlike gleam.

"I want what's mine," he said, stroking her lips with his fingers. "I belong inside your golden body, deep inside."

"Yes . . ." The sweet and urgent lassitude that had overtaken Honor was now flowing through her limbs, draining her of strength and will and reason. She clutched at his arms, startled when he caught hold of her hand and brought it to his mouth.

He kissed her fingertips, one by one, and then he breathed warm air into the hollow of her palm. "Touch me," he said, drawing her hand down his body to the heat of his loins. "Take me in your hand."

She did as he asked, caressing the hardness that sprang from his thighs. A sound of disbelief welled inside her. He was virile, quivering with life. Gingerly she stroked him, curling the tips of her fingers around the core of his male power, knowing that power would soon be entering her body.

"Honor," Johnny breathed huskily, "what are you doing to me?" He recoiled from her siren's touch. It was either that or lose control of himself in her hand.

"Why can't I touch you?" she asked, stroking his thigh.

Her fingers sent a shock wave of desire through him. He caught hold of her wrists and locked her hands above her head, forcing her flat to the ground. Stretched out beneath him like a captive maiden, she was irresistibly seductive. He lowered himself onto her gradually, loving the feel of his naked skin on hers, reveling in it. Her breasts spilled softly against his rib cage. Her loins melted under the heat of his weight. He could feel every wild beat of her pulse, every painful quiver of excitement.

"Because it's my turn," he said.

"Your turn for what?"

"To make you throb."

Holding her startled gaze, he ground his hips gently into hers and pressed the heat of his hardened shaft into her belly. She moaned at the pressure and tried to draw up her legs, but he kept her locked to the ground, pinned beneath him.

Merciless, he caught a tiny creamy piece of her throat between his teeth and nipped hard enough to make her shiver. A moment later he was biting her chin and watching her head arch back and her mouth come open. He'd never thought of himself as a voyeur, but he loved watching her respond when he did sensual things to her. He loved the helpless quiver of desire in her breathing.

"More," she whispered, shuddering.

"More what, Honor?"

She shook her head, refusing to say it.

"We've got a bargain, remember?" He held her wrists and slowly rotated against her, watching her gray eyes ignite with desire. He'd never felt anything more agonizingly sweet than the way her belly cradled his hardness. "Say it if you want it."

Her answer was lost in a throaty groan. She spread her legs beneath him, opening herself. Her hips lifted, wanton with the rhythms of love as she rubbed herself against him. He'd been wrong about it being his turn to make her throb. She had him coming out of his skin!

He moved alongside her and opened her thighs, caressing her with long, deep strokes. He wanted to arouse her in more intimate ways, to slide his fingers inside her, to taste her with his mouth. He wanted to be tender with her, slow and tender. More than anything he wanted that, but he was too hot, too hard. And she was too desirable.

He came up against her moist, tight opening. Pressing into her, he felt the velvet muscles begin to give way, yielding to him a little at a time. I'm home, he thought, his groin tightening.

"Yes, that," she moaned. "I want that."

He went still inside her, refusing to go any deeper. Searching her eyes, he saw how urgently she wanted him, but it wasn't enough. "No, you don't need that, Honor. You need me, inside you. Say it."

She dragged in a breath, struggling with the words. "I need you . . . inside me."

"No, say my name."

"Johnny!" she sobbed. "I need you, *Johnny*."

Her nails cut into his arm, and the pain enraged him, but it was more than a physical sensation. It was the tender rage of a man in need, in love. He could hardly bring himself to believe that she was lying beneath him, crying out his name as he entered her. He jerked with power of it, driving deeper inside her. The involuntary movement took control of his will, and he let go of all restraint, thrusting deeply, uncontrollably, with no thought but to take possession of every inch of her.

He breathed out her name as he came up against a fragile barrier and swept through it. His hardened shaft pressed into her with a will of its own, delving so deeply he could imagine coming up against her womb. The tight velvet resistance of her feminine walls seemed to stroke him, driving him on. It was the most wildly satisfying feeling he could ever re-member having.

"Take what's yours," she whispered, the words torn from her throat.

He began to rock into her, pounding out a rhythm that was as ancient as it was beautiful. She drew her legs up, absorbing him, whimpering with every new and deeper penetration. She clutched at his flanks when he slowed, as though she didn't want him to stop, but he had to. He needed to look at the woman in his arms, the golden girl he'd never stopped loving or hating.

Her eyes were bright with desire, dizzy with help-less pleasure. Her lips were swollen and languidly parted, crying out to be penetrated. He wanted her mouth, wanted it badly, but he didn't take it. There was something deep in her eyes that mesmerized him, something that made his heart contract. Did she feel the same way he did? Had she ever loved him the way he had her?

"Say my name," he rasped. "I need to hear you say it."

"Johnny."

"Again! Never stop saying it."

But Honor couldn't. She couldn't say anything more. He had begun to move deeply inside her again, and all she could do was moan tightly and clamp her thighs to his powerful hips as he brought her more pleasure than she'd ever known in her life. She murmured his name, and he swept her into his arms, shaking her body with near-violent thrusts. This was why she was alive, she realized, to be with Johnny, to make love with him and be loved by him, no matter how savagely.

"No!" she cried as he slowed once more.

He buried his hands in her hair, gentling her with his kisses. "I have to see this," he said. "I have to see us." When she'd quieted enough, he pushed up, supporting his weight with his arms. As he glanced down at the place where their bodies were joined, Honor realized what he was going to do, and it sent a forbidden thrill spiraling through her. He wanted to see himself making love to her.

He began to move, watching himself surge in and out of her body, and Honor began to climax.

"Hold me!" she cried.

He drove deeply, gathering her into his arms as waves of ecstasy washed over her. She clung to him, flew with him, pinwheeled through showers of feeling that left her breathless and stunned.

"Mine," he breathed with his last shuddering thrust into her woman's soul.

Ten

Johnny was absently aware of the birds chattering in the trees above them as he contemplated the beautiful, thoroughly ravished woman in his arms. "Can you handle a personal question?" he asked.

She laughed softly. "Anything but my weight or my age."

"How about your virginity?"

The smile vanished from her lips, and Johnny propped himself up on an elbow, studying her startled expression. "Honor, what we just did? You have done it before, haven't you?"

"Why do you ask?"

He was surprised at how defensive she seemed. He hadn't meant to embarrass her. "You seemed . . . tight, that's all."

She flushed and ducked her head, glancing up at him with the uncertain charm of that shy teenage girl he remembered. "Is that bad?" she asked. "To be ti—"

"No, it's not bad at all," he said, laughing. "It's wonderful, but I noticed some resistance, and I thought . . . I hope I didn't hurt you."

"You didn't," she said. "And I haven't."

"You haven't? *Never?*"

She shook her head. "I couldn't," she said. "I just couldn't. Not with anyone else."

He stared at her for a beat, trying to assimilate what she'd said. She'd never been with anyone else? Could that be true? Her expression was so open and guileless, he knew it must be. He gathered her up in his arms, his heart surging, his eyes squeezed shut. God, but this woman knew how to destroy him. He wanted to ask why she'd never been involved, but he could guess the answer. It had to be the same reason that all his sexual encounters had been virtually meaningless.

He drew back to look at her, astonished at the things he wanted to say to her and shaken by the force of his feelings. He felt as if something had given way inside him, as if some emotional safehold had broken open. He was filled with such beautiful, shattering needs. They scared the hell out of him, those needs.

"Johnny? Are you all right?"

He nodded slowly. "I should be asking you that."

"I'm fine," she assured him.

"Are you sure? Didn't you get . . ."—he searched for a word—"frustrated?"

"Well, yes," she admitted. "But I think now that it must have been some kind of self-imposed punishment. Like my hair. I never wore it down after you left. I wrapped it up in that tight little coil, and maybe I wrapped my other needs up with it."

Combing his hands into her tresses, Johnny brought the silky blondness forward and let it spill around her face. Her softness flowed all over his hands, as tender and surprising as the feelings flowing inside him. What had happened to the rage? he wondered. The need to inflict pain? He could hardly believe that all those years of cold hatred had been wiped out in one white-hot burst of passion. Was he really free of the demons? Clean?

He shook off the doubts, recapturing the magic of

her golden hair, lacing his fingers through the fine strands. All he seemed to want now was to be gentle with her. And to be buried deep inside her again. God, yes, he wanted that.

"The lady's first time," he said huskily. "If I were a gentleman, I wouldn't even suggest what's on my evil mind."

"Thank goodness you're not a gentleman."

He laughed and caressed her face with the silk entwined in his fingers. "I was thinking about how amazing it was. I was thinking about doing it to you again."

"Umm . . . yes," she breathed, her voice throaty. She reached up and began stroking her fingertips over his lips, thrilling him. "Do it to me again."

Johnny felt himself hardening like the granite peaks around them, though it seemed impossible he could get aroused again so quickly. He wanted to take it slower this time, to concentrate on her pleasure, but her fingers had a way of setting fire to whatever they touched. Their feathery lightness could ignite the most insatiable hunger.

"*Godistso*," he said, his voice going rough as he cupped her breast. "Love magic. You've put a spell on me, haven't you?"

He bent and took her mouth first, slowly, an animal growl in his throat. Leaving her lips wet and wanton, he moved to the breasts he'd claimed and began to suckle, pulling irresistibly on her tingling flesh. "I'm obsessed with a beautiful white witch," he said, glancing up at her with his hungry panther eyes. "Enslaved."

Honor dragged in a breath as his tongue flicked her nipple and brought it to quick, quivering tautness. "You?" she rasped, arching against his mouth. Each tug of his lips brought a sweet coiling tension to the pit of her stomach. She felt herself growing unbearably taut, as if the heavy satin ruffle she'd once imagined was being squeezed tighter and tighter. "I'm the one who's enslaved! What have you done to me?"

She caressed the darkness between his thighs, and he groaned out his need. He was hardened and quivering, ready for anything. She opened herself to him eagerly as he moved above her. Some terrible craving had taken over her will. He was big and thick and hot, and she needed him urgently. Her body was crying out to be filled, to be driven to the heights of ecstasy.

His eyes caught the light, flashing like a mercury as he entered her. He opened her up with a slow, deep stroke that made her plead for more. She moaned helplessly, imploring him to take her hard and fast. But he wouldn't give her the quick release she sought. He held himself in check, flexing inside her so slowly that she was nearly driven mad.

She raked her fingernails down his arm, opening the tender wound she'd made. "I'm sorry!" she cried, but it was too late.

"Witch," he breathed, thrusting into her deeply, shuddering as the rage overtook him. He was a man possessed. He drove into her with passionate force, again and again, bringing her the most incredible rapture imaginable. He shook her to her core, but it wasn't enough. The rage was in him, demanding satisfaction.

He rolled her over on her stomach and pulled her up on all fours, thrusting into that tender, aching part of her body, violating her with his beautiful darkness. Honor moaned and cried, paralyzed with pleasure as his thrusts shook through her, thrilling her. Even in her dazed state, she understood what had happened. The panther had taken possession of her. She had unleashed the dark feral animal, and he would either devour her with his passion or drive her to the heights of ecstasy.

• • •

*The arrow struck its target with a piercing sound.
The wounded hawk unfurled its wings, creating a
magnificent cape of white, then transforming before
his eyes into a hauntingly beautiful woman. The cape
fell away, and her long golden hair flew around her,
exposing her nakedness. A look of anguish clouded
her exquisite eyes. She was bleeding. The arrow had
pierced her heart, and the life force was ebbing from
her in a bright crimson ribbon. She was dying. . . .*

Johnny woke up drenched in sweat. Honor was
slumped against him, and he pulled her closer, certain that she'd been mortally wounded. She moaned
softly and nuzzled into the warmth of his shoulder,
sound asleep but very much alive.

Sighing with relief, he buried a hand in her hair
and held her tightly to his chest. The emotions
storming through him were chaotic and confused,
but the dream had been terrifyingly real. He'd seen
every detail with a clarity that had frightened the hell
out of him. He'd even seen the color of the woman's
eyes, blue-gray like river mist. Honor's eyes.

He pulled her dress around her to protect her from
the cold. She slept on undisturbed in his arms, and
Johnny envied her tranquillity. He had no such
peace of mind. As he lay there, holding her in the
darkness, sheltered only by the remains of the lean-
to, he had the eeriest feeling that he was still caught
in a surreal dreamscape.

It seemed as if he had never come out of the
nightmare, as if everything that had happened on
the mountain the last few days was a part of it,
including the sex they'd had before falling asleep
tonight. Had his grandfather cast some kind of spell
over them? Had that crazy old man invoked the
powers of *godistso*?

He could hardly believe he was considering the
possibility, but he didn't know how else to explain

the insanity his life had become. He'd spent half his life trying to forget her and bring his emotions under control. But the instant she reappeared, he'd been twisted inside out. Even now he was so torn with conflicting emotion, he hardly knew how he felt.

Beyond that he'd broken every promise he'd made to himself. Years ago, he'd sworn he would never return to the reservation. Then, just days ago, he'd sworn that the woman who'd betrayed him would hurt the way he had hurt. All that was inconceivable to him now that he was on the reservation, seeking the ways of his Apache ancestors, and the very woman he'd vowed to get even with was curled up naked in his arms.

Had the whole world gone crazy?

He held Honor tight to his chest, his hands tangled in the golden magic of her hair. It would all be so simple if he could blame everything on the bewitching creature in his arms, but he couldn't do that. He'd made the choice to be with her again, however recklessly.

All he'd wanted when he returned to this place was to free himself. Instead, he'd added more chains, he realized. Loving her promised to be infinitely more dangerous than hating her. Even the vengeance he thought would cleanse him had turned into something complicated, tainted by guilt and remorse. To hurt her now would make him a monster. He would never be able to live with himself. But to love her?

When Honor woke up the next morning, Johnny had already dismantled their primitive camp and was ready to make the trip back to the reservation.

"Hungry?" he asked, settling down next to her with a bark bowl of wild strawberries and artichoke roots.

"Maybe I'd better get dressed first," said Honor,

aware that she was naked under the blouse and skirt that covered her. Despite their intimacy of the night before, she felt oddly vulnerable with him sitting right next to her. Maybe it was *because* of their intimacy, she realized, blushing as she remembered what they'd done. His animal passions had awakened and aroused her in ways she wouldn't have believed possible. She was already throbbing just thinking about it.

She sneaked a glance at his naked thighs and felt herself going weak all over. Heaven help her, she wanted him again! Now, deep and tender, hot inside her. Her stomach muscles clutched in anticipation of the forbidden pleasure, but she couldn't let him know how much she had loved what he'd done to her. She couldn't embarrass herself that way!

She hurriedly dressed, and the activity calmed her a little, though her panties and bra were nowhere to be found. Then she shared breakfast with him, nibbling at the roots he offered, absently aware that they reminded her of jicama. Her mind wasn't on food, however.

"I was hoping we could talk," she said.

"I was hoping we wouldn't," he told her softly.

"What's wrong?"

His eyes glinted darkly, beautifully, simmering with inner turmoil as he looked at her. "It's too soon. I'm not up to a whole lot of soul-searching this morning. I'm still trying to deal with what happened last night."

"Soul-searching?" Honor blurted out the offending word, unable to hide her hurt. "That wasn't what I had in mind." She stopped herself with a sigh and looked away from him. Soul-searching was exactly what she had in mind. "You're right," she said. "Maybe it is too soon."

Silence stretched between them until Johnny finally broke it. "I'm sorry, baby. I really am." He knew he'd hurt her. He could see it in her proud, unsteady chin. But how did he tell her what was going on when he couldn't find the words to explain it to himself? He'd been ripped wide open last night. He was too exposed, too raw, for any more contact. He wanted like hell to drag her into his arms and make love to her again. He could lose himself in her, but talking would only stir up all the pain and confusion. Talking was dangerous.

"Maybe we ought to get going," she said finally. "It's a long trip back."

Honor's prediction was too modest. It was a torturous trip back. Neither she nor Johnny spoke except when necessary, but Honor couldn't stop herself from trying to analyze his every mood, every glance and murmur. She tried to tell herself that she was only imagining the distance seeping back into his eyes, the walls going up. She prayed she was imagining it, but she couldn't talk herself out of the gnawing fear that he was retreating to somewhere beyond her reach.

If she had any sense, she'd be the one retreating.

She wiped the moisture from her neck and forehead as they continued down the mountain, but she couldn't pry her thoughts away from the man walking next to her. His silence fed into her anxieties. It was more painful than his anger. At least then he was involved with her, passionately involved.

She knew he could hurt her. He could crush her emotionally simply by his indifference. She was too vulnerable to him now, too needy for any scraps of attention or tenderness he might throw her way. And he had too many reasons to want to crush her. He'd threatened revenge, and the shaman had warned her she would be hurt. Was this what the old man meant?

By the time the town of Whiteriver came into view, Honor had withdrawn into herself emotionally. She was afraid of Johnny's moody silences, of his seemingly fated need to wound her. The shaman had told her she would learn something on the mountain, but nothing could have been further from the truth. She was hopelessly mired in confusion. Why had she and Johnny been brought together at all if it was only to cause each other more pain?

The first person Honor saw as she and Johnny walked into the tribal headquarters in Whiteriver was the blond-haired ruffian. The man who had spied on her at the river was actually standing across the room, talking to Johnny's grandfather! *"You?"* she said, halting midstride. "What are you doing here?"

The ruffian's gaze swept over her, and he smiled roguishly. "Ask your friend," he said, indicating Johnny.

Johnny's malevolent expression made Honor think the men must be dire enemies. "You said you didn't know him," she whispered to Johnny.

"I wish I didn't," Johnny muttered, swinging an arm toward the man. "Honor, meet Geoff Dias, my partner in another life. You may remember calling him to do some investigating for us."

"Your partner?" Honor gazed at Geoff in surprise, letting herself get caught for an instant in the man's rich green eyes and sensual smile. He virtually lit up the room with his potent male energy, and even Honor, with all her other preoccupations, was not immune.

The awareness left Honor worried as she caught the homicidal glint in Johnny's eyes. He was measuring his former partner's jaw for a fist, she realized, and the last thing she wanted was two bad-tempered brutes going at each other in the tribal headquarters. Still, Johnny's jealousy was flattering, she admitted. It reassured her that he hadn't been able to turn himself off totally. If she hadn't been afraid of provoking a fight, she might have rattled his cage a little harder.

"We have important business at hand," Chy Star-hawk said, interrupting in the nick of time.

The urgency in his tone drew Honor's attention to the small crowd of tribal leaders gathered in the room. Their grave expressions startled her into re-membering that there was something more at stake here than her own personal concerns. These people were fighting to protect their tribe's livelihood and a young boy's freedom.

Standing beside the shaman was the accused Apache teenager whose bail Honor had helped ar-range. Her heart went out to the boy. His long black hair and look of defiance reminded her of another teenager who'd gone up against the system once and lost.

"Mr. Dias has uncovered some important evidence regarding the Bartholomew Mines," the shaman said, nodding to Geoff.

The room went still as Geoff described the discrep-ancies he'd found in the chemical analyses of the seepage from the holding ponds. "Not only were the reports falsified," he told them as he finished his disclosures, "they were signed off on by a govern-ment inspector, which could mean any number of things—bribery, graft, collusion."

The crowd broke out in applause.

"But that's perfect!" Honor chimed in. "You have everything we need. We can have the operation shut down, at least until they rectify the situation. How did you ever get past my father's security?"

Geoff pulled a card from the pocket of his vest. "Anyone need a computer repaired? I work cheap. Once I was able to access their locked electronic files, I hit pay dirt."

"Brilliant," said Honor, laughing along with every-one else. But her smile vanished as Johnny inter-rupted.

"There's a problem," he said, addressing the tribal leaders. He gave Honor the benefit of his quick, hot glare as he indicated Geoff. "Mr. Dias's 'brilliant' evidence was illegally obtained. Technically he gained access to the computer files by fraudulent means, which makes the evidence virtually worthless in court. And leaves us with damn few options."

The crowd began to murmur among themselves.

"What are those options?" Chy Starhawk asked immediately.

Johnny's shrug wasn't encouraging. "We either find someone within the company to testify that the analyses were falsified, which is an unlikely prospect . . . or we bluff."

"Bluff?"

It was Honor who'd asked the question, but Johnny addressed his answer to the men, pointedly ignoring her. "Hale Bartholomew doesn't have to know how we got the evidence," he told them. "We could bluff him into thinking we can win a court fight."

Chy Starhawk looked skeptical. "There is too much at stake," he said. "Do we want the boy's future and our tribe's livelihood hanging on so thin a thread?"

"I think we could do it," Honor said softly, more to herself than anyone else. Her thoughts began to race as she considered the possibilities. She didn't question that what Johnny proposed was a huge risk, but she'd seen the flame leap in his eyes when he said her father's name. Johnny Starhawk and Hale Bartholomew? A confrontation after so many years between the half-Apache kid and the man who had him banished? It was poetic justice, she realized.

She came out of her thoughts to the realization that everyone was looking at her, including Johnny. "I . . . I think we could do it," she repeated. "I know my father. He's been railing for years about the environmentalists and how they value trees over people. His motives aren't always as pure as he pretends, but he does put great store in the family name and his own integrity. If we threatened public exposure—"

"What if it came to a court fight?" Johnny asked. "Would you testify against him? A character witness?"

"Testify?" Honor whispered the word. "Against my own father?" She stared at Johnny in disbelief. Did he know what he was asking? Her relationship with her father wasn't a good one, but to publically take the stand against him? She could never do it. There was a bond. There would always be a bond.

She searched Johnny's features, trying to understand what he was doing, why he was doing it. Her father had used her as a pawn all those years ago. He'd forced her to choose between him and Johnny. It horrified her to think that Johnny might be doing the same thing now. That would be carrying poetic justice to its cruelest extreme.

Her throat was dry and sore as she tried to speak. "Maybe it won't come to a court fight."

"If it did?" Johnny persisted.

Don't do this, she thought, her anguish evident as she held his gaze. *Please, don't do this.*

The silence stretched interminably, and finally Johnny exhaled heavily, his head lifting. He turned to his grandfather. "I'm ready to take Bartholomew on, with or without her. You decide."

As Johnny turned and headed for the door, the assembled group made way for him. Honor felt as if she were drowning, going down for the third time, and Johnny had turned his back on her struggle. The door banged shut behind him, and she walked to the window of the headquarters, watching him stride to his Jeep.

"He'll be back," a man's voice said reassuringly.

She turned to find Geoff Dias standing next to her.

"Johnny's a moody S.O.B.," Geoff said, his expression conveying sympathy for her plight. "But he'll work through whatever's eating him. Give him some time."

Honor shook her head. Geoff obviously had no idea

how serious the situation was. "It's more than a mood," she said despairingly. "Johnny can't let go of the past, and he's determined to punish me for it, one way or the other."

Geoff moved around her and settled himself on the ledge of the window, looking up at her, studying her sadness. The light caught his sunswept hair and made a fiery halo out of it. He looked like one of Satan's angels, Honor thought.

His voice was husky when he spoke. "I'll tell you a little secret," he said. "I've seen Johnny around lots of women, but I've never seen him like this. I don't think punishing you is his problem. I think it's loving you."

Honor saw the bonfire as she was walking toward the river the town was named for. Blazing against the summer evening's darkness, it seemed to be somewhere in the fairgrounds. She hurried in that direction, thinking that the fire might be another ceremonial ritual, perhaps in preparation for the confrontation with her father. If she was lucky, the person she needed to see would be there.

She approached the fairgrounds expecting the same crowds she'd seen at the *gaan* dance. Instead the area was deserted. There was only one man sitting cross-legged before the fire. Johnny's grandfather rocked in a trancelike state, staring into the soul of the flames, chanting softly.

Honor hesitated a few feet away, not wanting to disturb him, but the shaman seemed to sense her presence and looked up. His eyes reflected the flames. They warmed and chilled her at the same time.

"You're troubled," he said.

"Very troubled," she admitted.

"Do you know why?" he asked, beckoning her to sit down.

"Yes," she said, speaking with conviction as she

settled herself next to him on the ground. "It's your grandson. I don't understand him."

"You aren't alone. He doesn't understand himself."

"But why is he doing this?" she persisted. "Why is he asking me to testify against my own father?"

"Perhaps because he wants to win the case, and he knows you would be an important witness."

She sighed and shook her head. "If I could believe that was all there was to it—"

The fire snapped loudly, showering sparks. Several of them hit Honor's sweatshirt, and as she hastened to pat them out, she noticed the shaman's bare arm. It was covered with red-hot cinders, which he made no move to extinguish. The cinders turned to ash, and as she met the old man's eyes, she saw herself there, reflected in the fire's flames. The vision transfixed her for a moment, as though there were some secret truth hidden in his gaze.

"You mistrust Johnny's motives?" he asked.

"Yes, I do," she said. "I think it's a test. If I pass it, maybe he'll forgive me. Or maybe there'll be another test."

The shaman smiled. "You are becoming a wise woman."

Her pleasure at the compliment flared and was gone, like the sparks. "Then you think it's a test too?"

"Does it matter? If it is, you couldn't pass it. You already know that, so you might as well search your heart and look for guidance there."

Search her heart? Wasn't that exactly what she'd been doing? "You told me I would learn something on the trip to White Mountain, and yet I came back feeling more confused than ever."

"And now? You're still confused? You feel helpless, a leaf in the wind?"

"Yes . . ." How did he know?

"And perhaps you feel Johnny is that wind? A

stormy gust, battering at you?" As she nodded, he asked, "Do you know the wind's purpose?"

"To rip the leaf from the tree, to destroy it."

"Ah, but is the leaf destroyed when it's ripped from the tree? Or is it taken on a great ride, a great adventure? Some leaves might see the wind as an opportunity to travel."

He laughed softly at that thought and regarded her with curiosity. "What do you want from the wind, little leaf?"

Honor smiled despite herself. "I'd like a trip with less turbulence, thank you."

"So you want a gentle wind, a loving wind?"

She nodded, stirred by bittersweet feelings. Gentleness, love—she longed for those things. She longed for Johnny's love.

"Have you told him how you feel?" the shaman asked.

Honor glanced up, startled. The fire turned to liquid gold through the haze of her tears. "No, I'd be afraid to tell him," she admitted softly. "Everything I do seems to hurt and enrage him. He can't let himself forget, or forgive, what I did."

"Yes, I see that," the shaman said gently. "But perhaps it isn't Johnny's pain you need to be concerned with. And perhaps it isn't Johnny's forgiveness you need."

Honor stared into his eyes, into the flames, and saw herself there, waiting, hoping, fearful, a leaf about to be torn from the tree. The suffering in her own gaze mesmerized her. It spoke to her heart. "It's myself I must forgive?" she asked after a moment.

"Yes, leaf, forgive yourself, for everything. That is the only way you will ever be free to go where the wind takes you. That is how you become the wind."

Eleven

Johnny stood in the open doorway of the small roadside tavern, leaning against the doorframe and looking out at nothing in particular, a longneck bottle of beer in his hand. Flashes of light from down the road and the thunder of an approaching motorcycle told him that his already lousy evening had just taken a turn for the worst. Trouble was headed his way.

The Harley Low Rider that roared up to the tavern entrance and stopped inches from Johnny's feet was one of the toughest, sexiest machines he'd ever seen. The bike had more custom chrome and iron than a Grand Prix Ferrari race car. Johnny couldn't help but appreciate the cycle. Its rider was another matter. He wanted no part of Geoff Dias at the moment.

Geoff rolled the bike back from the entrance, hit the kickstand, and swung off. "Hardly recognized you with your clothes on," he said, tossing off the wisecrack as he brushed past Johnny and entered the tavern.

A moment later he came back through the doorway with a can of beer and an inquisitive expression that was trying to pretend it wasn't a smart-ass grin. Settling himself opposite Johnny, he leaned against the tavern's log-cabin exterior and propped a booted foot on the wall behind him. "You okay?" he asked, taking a deep swig from the can.

"I didn't know you cared," Johnny said dryly. "I feel as though I've been hung head down over a slow fire and roasted for days on end. Other than that, I'm great."

Geoff gave out a low whistle of sympathy. "How'd you get yourself into this mess?"

"I think you got a pretty good look at the reason, you slimy bastard—Honor Bartholomew, star of my teenage fantasies and bane of my entire existence. That's how I got into this mess."

"Does the bane of your existence know you're nuts about her?"

Johnny drained the bottle. "She knows I'm nuts."

Geoff's handsome features were uncharacteristically serious as he rested the back of his head against the log cabin, then glanced around at Johnny. "Why do you want to hurt her, man? What's that going to prove?"

Johnny stared at the empty beer bottle, wishing he could smash it against something just for the pleasure of seeing it explode. "I don't want to hurt her. Not anymore. I want it over, that's all. I just want it over."

"You may be about to get your wish."

"Get my wish? Why?" Johnny pushed away from the door and scrutinized his ex-partner as if Geoff had announced that Honor were terminally ill and about to depart the planet. "Did she say something? Is she leaving? Where is she?"

"You're really pathetic, man," Geoff said, his voice husky with pained male laughter. "You've got it bad."

Johnny tapped the empty bottle against the palm of his hand, fighting off the desire to use Geoff's skull for target practice. The crazy Indian's got it bad, he thought. Might as well hire a skywriter instead of trying to keep that fact under wraps. "I need a drink," he said, turning to go into the bar.

"You don't need a drink," Geoff said forcefully. He pushed off the wall and confronted Johnny, apparently prepared to knock heads if that's what it took. "You need to grow up, buddy. You saved my butt when those rebels ambushed me in Peru, and I never thought I'd hear myself calling you a coward. But I'm awful close to it now. If you love her, Starhawk, if you want the woman, then stop jacking around and do something about it."

Johnny stared at his friend incredulously. "You just made a couple of big mistakes, Dias," he said softly. "The first one is getting in my face. You oughta know better than that. The second is being right. *I hate it when you're right.*"

Johnny spotted her the moment he came out of the Sunrise Motel the next morning. Honor was leaning against his Jeep Cherokee, looking squarely at him, her arms folded casually, her hair bleached to white in the dazzling sunlight. At first glance she looked like one of those visions that came to a man in his hour of need, an angel of mercy or a genie materializing out of a bottle.

At second glance she looked like a woman who had something serious in mind. The blue blazer, skirt, and blouse she wore were all business, and the set of her lovely jaw bespoke determination.

Johnny dug his car keys from the pocket of his suit jacket. "I've got business," he said by way of explanation. It was true, but it was also a convenient way to postpone whatever kind of confrontation she had on her mind.

"I know," she said, remaining where she was, blocking the driver's side of the car.

"My business is with your father."

"You have an appointment?"

"Not exactly. His secretary referred me to his attorneys, but that's never stopped me before. I'm pretty good at crashing gates."

"That's why I'm here," she informed him. "I'm going with you. At least my being there will ensure that he sees you."

"Honor, you don't have to—"

She cut him off with a toss of her head. "I'm not doing it for you, Starhawk, and I don't need your permission one way or the other, is that clear?"

"Abundantly," he said softly as he stared at her sparkling eyes and expressive mouth. "Starhawk? You've never called me that before."

"Be glad I did," she said. "The other names I had in mind aren't nearly as polite."

Against his better judgment, Johnny realized he was fascinated. He'd always thought her fair complexion and her genteel shyness were what gave her her unique quality of beauty, but she seemed to be operating from a completely different energy source now. She was lighting up the motel's dingy parking lot with her heat and flash.

Once, caught in the throes of his own insanity and frustration, he'd heard a word shaking on his lips when he'd been about to kiss her. He'd called her a bitch, but his fury had been mixed with awe even then. She gave new meaning to that pejorative term now. She was fabulous.

"Let's get going," he said. "I'm driving."

Triumph shimmered in her smile. "If you insist."

The trip to Phoenix, where Hale Bartholomew's corporate offices were located, was made in deafening silence, interrupted by occasional uneasy attempts at conversation on Johnny's part. He'd never been more aware of Honor's presence than in the enforced confinement of the rented Jeep. He was aware of her hips as she moved in the bucket seat, of her hands clasped in her lap, and especially of her legs rustling around in the skirt she wore. What was it about a short skirt and silk stockings that made a woman's legs look sleek and never-ending? His thoughts veered irresistibly to the night he'd opened those sleek legs.

A blaring car horn brought him out of his fantasy, but not quickly enough to stop the surge of energy in his loins. "Sorry," he muttered, bringing the Jeep back into the lane he'd veered out of.

"Is there a problem?" Honor asked, surprised at the heated glance he gave her. She was equally aware of their tight quarters and of Johnny's presence. Though his hair was tied back in a ponytail, it did little to subdue the animal magnetism he exuded, and neither did the business suit he wore. It astonished her that a pair of men's linen slacks could be so blatantly sexy. And it annoyed her that she couldn't keep her eyes off his hand as he worked the car's stick shift!

"Hell, yes, there's a problem," he said huskily, gearing down as a car pulled in front of them. "Isn't there always?"

Honor swayed toward him, her leg colliding with the very hand she'd been watching. The friction of silk sliding along bare skin created sparks of static that traveled up her thigh like an electrical charge. She jerked back and returned his heated glance, determined not to respond to him. But her mind had other ideas. It flashed X-rated images of a man sliding his hand up a woman's skirt, of steamy sex in parked cars.

"Is there a problem?" he asked, his smile darkly ironic as he echoed her words.

As they approached the outskirts of Phoenix, Honor forced her thoughts to the ordeal that lay ahead of them, the confrontation with her father. She'd sent Christmas and birthday cards, but other than that she'd had no contact with Hale Bartholomew in over a decade, and she was terribly nervous. He was a powerful man. He was intelligent, articulate, ruthless—all those qualities she'd seen in Johnny the first time she'd watched him argue a case. But her father had the hometown advantage of having friends in high places. He also believed passionately in his principles, however misguided others might think they were. She wasn't sure even Johnny could win against such a man.

"What's your plan for dealing with my father?" she asked as they pulled into the parking lot of the Bartholomew Building.

"I'm going to play it by ear, look for his weakest link. The public-exposure angle could work."

"That was my idea," she said, surprised.

He acknowledged her with a faint smile. "Yes, I know."

Moments later, having maneuvered their way past the ground-floor security, Honor and Johnny stepped off the executive elevator and faced their second hurdle, the receptionist.

"She couldn't be any worse than your receptionist," Honor told Johnny under her breath as they approached the woman's desk. "Hello, I'm Honor Bartholomew," she said, smiling pleasantly. "Mr. Bartholomew's daughter."

The young woman looked startled. "His daughter? Do you have an appointment?"

Honor ignored the question. "Is he alone?" she asked, glancing at the vaultlike double doors.

The receptionist rose protectively. "Yes, but he's busy. If you'll have a seat, I'll let him know you're here."

"Not necessary," Honor said breezily, waving Johnny along with her. "We want to surprise him."

The double doors led to a hallway of executive offices. Carried along by her own boldness and ignoring the receptionist's calls to stop, Honor moved swiftly toward her father's suite at the end of the hall. Fortunately she remembered the way.

Hale Bartholomew hung up the telephone as she

and Johnny entered. "Honor?" he said, rising. "What are you doing here?"

Honor hadn't realized how hard her heart was thumping until she stopped and caught her breath. All the starch and stiffness seemed to drain out of her as she came face-to-face with her tall, distinguished father. He looked even more aged and gaunt than he had on television. "Can we talk to you, Father?" she asked.

"What is it?" he demanded, obviously surprised and reluctant. "Why didn't you call?"

"I thought you might refuse to see us." Honor searched the lines and furrows of her father's craggy face for any indication of his feelings. She knew he'd turned things around in his mind when she left. He'd made her the guilty party, the thankless child abandoning a well-meaning parent. Her father had always been a master at revising life to suit his purposes, and yet she wanted to believe her leaving had affected him in some way.

She felt her resolve collapsing under his silent scrutiny. After so many years of trying to win his love and approval, she would have thought herself immune, but clearly she wasn't. She searched his slate-gray eyes for any signs of acceptance. Was he at all glad to see her?

"Who's this with you?" he asked, turning his attention to Johnny.

"You remember Johnny Starhawk," Honor said tentatively.

Her father's face went slack with surprise, but Johnny nodded to the older man as if he hadn't noticed. He didn't seem the slightest bit ruffled by her formidable father. On the contrary, he looked as though he might even be relishing the oncoming battle.

"Johnny's going to be representing the Apache teenager who's been charged with sabotaging the mine," Honor explained.

Hale's eyes glittered with anger. "Honor, this is outrageous! I'm not going to jeopardize the state's case by talking to the boy's attorney, I don't care who he is!"

He turned his wrath on Johnny next. "I think you'd better get out of here, young man. Immediately!"

"Father—"

"It's all right, Honor," Johnny said. "I've grown up a little since the last time your father kicked my butt out of town. He's not going to do it again." He turned to her father. "If you don't want to hear what I've got to say, Mr. Bartholomew, there are plenty of people who do, including the media."

"Are you threatening me?" Hale blustered.

"Don't think of it as a threat," Johnny said calmly. "Think of it as an ironclad contract. I've got all the evidence I need to close your operation down indefinitely—fraudulent chemical analyses, falsified reports, numbers doctored to meet government standards." He drew the photocopied reports from his briefcase and handed them to Hale.

Honor watched with alarm as her father read the reports. His face was blotched with angry color, and when he glanced up, his voice was raspy. "Where did you get these?" he demanded to know. "From someone on my office staff?"

Johnny closed his briefcase quietly. "I don't reveal my sources. But if I were you, I'd think twice about letting this fight go public."

"I didn't falsify those reports," Bartholomew said harshly. "And I don't know who did."

"Of course, you didn't," Johnny cut back. "We know how that works, don't we? You guys at the top never get your hands dirty. You have some minion to take care of the problem, and you let him know you don't care *how* he gets it done. Right?"

As if declaring war, the older man crushed the reports in his hand and threw them in his wastebasket. "Don't underestimate me, young man," he warned. "That would be a serious mistake."

Johnny lifted his head, his eyes catching the glare from the window. "The mistake has already been made, Mr. Bartholomew, and it's going to cost you dearly. The toxins seeping from your holding pool are poisoning the reservation's pasturelands. The tribe's livelihood is being destroyed, and it's just a matter of time before human health is affected, if it hasn't been already. The personal damage suits alone will bankrupt you."

"It would take an act of God to bankrupt me, Starhawk."

"Maybe that can be arranged."

The two men locked eyes for a moment, and Johnny knew he was dealing with a worthy adversary. Hale Bartholomew might be past his physical prime, but he was as mentally sharp and cunning as ever. The man was a gut-fighter.

"There's more than just the dollar cost," Johnny said. "The tribe will be perceived as victims, and the media blitz will turn public opinion in their favor. Activists from all over the country will haunt you, Mr. Bartholomew. They'll picket your home and all your other business interests, not just the mine. They'll turn your life into one long protest rally from hell."

"Are you done?" Bartholomew asked.

"No," Johnny said, "I'm just getting started. If you don't clean up your act where the mine's concerned, compensate the tribe for their losses, and arrange to have the charges dismissed against the boy, I'm going to have plenty more to say, in court."

The older man hit an ornate brass humidor on his desk, banging the lid with a loud crack. "My daughter should have warned you that I don't respond well to intimidation tactics, Mr. Starhawk. If you think you can beat me in court, then why are you here now? Tipping your hand, I might add."

"I'm here to save us all some grief, Mr. Bartholomew. A court fight will be time-consuming and costly."

"I have plenty of time and money," the older man snapped. "Do your clients?"

Honor stepped forward, appalled at what was happening. They were going at each other verbally like two pit bulls. "Father, for heaven's sake, accept his terms," she urged. "I've seen the reports. Whether or not you had anything to do with them, your company did, and you're responsible. The mine is polluting reservation land. Why can't you just admit it?"

She drew in a breath as she met his stony gaze, and her voice began to tremble. "Why can't you do the right thing for once?"

He leaned forward on his desk, his arms unsteady. "You walked out of my life a long time ago, Honor. That act stripped you of any right to preach to me about ethics. I won't have you marching into my office haranguing me about my responsibilities, do you hear me?"

"Yes, I hear you." Honor felt a surge of hurt and fury. How many times had she answered him with exactly those words? How many times had she swallowed whatever she'd needed to say because he wouldn't allow her to speak?

Johnny touched her arm, but she waved him off.

"Yes, I did hear you," she repeated with quiet force as she approached her father's desk. "Now you hear me, dammit. If you don't accept Johnny's terms, and this case goes to court, I will be up there on the stand, testifying against you."

"Honor, don't be ridiculous. You can't—"

"Yes!" she said, "I can, and I will."

"You don't know what you're doing!"

"I know how you make deals, Father. Did you forget that I was there when you invited the judge to dinner after Johnny'd been sent away? I heard the two of you congratulating each other on your cleverness at having Johnny's sentence dismissed on the condition that he leave town. The judge received an important appointment that same year, didn't he?"

Her father stared at her in shock, the color slowly draining from his face. He slumped into his chair, and for a moment Honor was frightened for his health.

"How could you do this?" he asked her, indicating Johnny. "How could you align yourself with *him*?"

Honor heard the prejudice in his tone, but instead of anger, she felt pity. Her father's world was so narrow. Her twin brother was the only one who had ever been able to please him, and that was because he'd made Hale, Jr., into a replica of himself. Perhaps she was fortunate to have escaped her father's love.

"Good God, child," Hale Bartholomew said. "All these years and you still haven't come to your senses?"

"No, you're quite wrong, Father," she said, all the anger gone out of her. "I have come to my senses, just this moment." It was true, she realized. Several insights had come upon her in the last few moments, stunning insights about herself, her father, and Johnny.

Summoning courage, she prepared herself to deal with the two most difficult and intimidating men in her life. "I'm in love with Johnny," she said with uncharacteristic bluntness. "I've always loved him. I'm even thinking of asking him to marry me."

Honor hazarded a glance at Johnny and saw that he'd gone nearly as pale as her father. Neither man said a word. She seemed to have rendered them both speechless. It was Honor's first real taste of her own power, and it hit her in such a dizzying rush, she almost smiled.

Aware of her father's stricken expression, she felt a welling sympathy. "I know you can't understand this, but it's what I truly want, and it's taken me a long time to find the courage to say it." There was something else she needed to say. "I love you, Father," she told him softly. "In spite of everything, I always have. All I ever wanted was your love and approval when I was a child, but I realize now that I don't need either to survive. Still, I hope someday we'll learn to understand and accept our differences, and perhaps even build a bridge back to each other."

She hesitated, saddened when her father couldn't seem to bring himself to look up at her. She stepped back from both men and saw that Johnny couldn't look at her either. He seemed completely preoccupied, as if he'd vanished into some inner world. Either he was still thunderstruck, or he simply hadn't wanted to hear what she had to say. Suddenly her father's spacious office seemed small and claustrophobic.

"Make the right decision about the mine, Father," she said, brushing past Johnny as she left.

Moments later she was across the street from the Bartholomew Building, walking in the same park she and Hale, Jr., had played in as children. The sky was a sharp cerulean blue, and the breezes rustling through the trees overhead made it an unusually mild day for midsummer.

Honor stopped at the edge of a small fountain, remembering how Hale had gone wading there once and been caught by their father. Hale had cried and immediately been forgiven. Honor, of course, wouldn't have thought to disobey in the first place. Things had changed drastically, she realized. She didn't regret a word of what she'd said in her father's office. It had been imperative that she tell him how she felt. She'd had to open her heart where both men were concerned, even if it meant losing them.

"Honor?"

It was Johnny's voice, but she didn't turn, afraid to face him. She felt almost clairvoyant where he was concerned, as if she were able to read the future in his eyes. One look and she would know everything.

"The lady seems a little tense," he said, coming up behind her. "I'll bet she could use a massage?"

"Massage?" Had she heard him correctly? He actually sounded as if he might be smiling, having fun with her. She didn't know whether to be relieved or angry. "If the lady were any more tense, she'd be one of the park's statues. I think it's going to take more than a massage, thank you."

"What is it going to take?"

His voice stirred her senses like the wind rifling through the trees overhead. His hand stroked down her arm and caught hold of the fist she'd clasped against her stomach. He covered it and brought her up against him, holding her gently, breathing warmth into her hair.

"This could work," she allowed.

He felt wonderful, as warm and enveloping as the night he'd held her on the mountain. She closed her eyes, wishing as she had then that she could be absorbed into his heat, drawn into his sheltering male strength like a kitten tucked away in a pocket. She didn't want to move, to think, or even to breathe, for fear that she might lose the beautiful feelings he brought her.

"Honor, you said some things in there, and I—" He hesitated, clearing the graininess from his throat. "I know you were angry at your father, but I wondered if you meant all of that . . . or any of it?"

Was he stumbling over the words? She thanked God at that moment that she wasn't looking a him. Surely he would have seen the astonishment in her eyes. She never thought she would live long enough to hear Johnny Starhawk fumble his lines. She must really have blown some circuits with her proposal.

"Honor?" he pressed, his arm tightening around her middle. "Did you?"

"Did I what?"

"Did you mean it?"

A terrible impulse came over her. She wanted to do

something she wouldn't have believed herself capable of. She wanted to keep him dangling. "That I loved my father?" she said softly, wickedly. "Of course I meant it."

The muscles of his arm tautened. She could feel the heat of his body burning through her clothing. She could hear his impatient exhalation and knew she was in trouble. Wonderful trouble!

He turned her in his arms, whirling her so possessively, she was breathless and dizzy as he caught her up against him. The dark flames leaped in his eyes. His gaze burned as hotly as ever, but there was love in its heat, tenderness.

"Didn't anybody ever teach you not to tease the animals in the zoo?" he warned. A sexy growl rumbled in his throat as he curved his hand to her throat. "Despite your efforts, this one isn't quite tamed or domesticated yet."

"And never will be," she conceded, a thrill spiraling up from the depths of her. "Despite my efforts." She touched his mouth, her fingers trembling over its fine sensuality. "Yes, I meant it, every word. I love you, Johnny. I always have."

He smiled with effort, as if his jaw had suddenly locked. "Forgive me if I'm having some trouble with this," he said. "I never thought it could happen." His laughter had an aching sound. "Are you sure? You actually want to marry me? A crazy Irish-Apache lawyer?"

"It's the lawyer part I'm worried about."

He shook his head, disbelieving. "As long as you know what you're getting into. I'm not an easy man to live with. I'm prone to jealous rages, and I'll probably do terrible things to you, just like in the mountains."

"Oh! I'm looking forward to it!"

His jaw locked again, and his dark eyes flared with pain and passion. "I love you, baby."

She gazed up at him, her chin trembling, her heart so full she couldn't speak a word.

Johnny knew the sweetest kind of agony as he pulled her into his arms and rocked her. She felt like heaven, or all he would ever know of that perfect place. She was the girl of his dreams, the woman of his heart. Maybe this was destiny playing itself out in his life in some inexplicable way. He didn't know. But whatever was happening, it was bigger than his puny doubts and fears. He knew legal procedure like the back of his hand, but there was so much he didn't understand about life, things like forgiveness, tolerance, and humility. Maybe he was supposed to learn those things . . . from her.

"Let's have kids," he said, holding her back.

"Oh, yes! Beautiful Irish-Apache babies with dark eyes."

"No way," he countered, laughing huskily. "Dimpled cherubs with golden hair and misty blue eyes." *He loved her.* Nothing could alter that irrefutable fact. He loved her like nothing else in this world, with every cell of his heart and mind.

A leaf spiraled down from one of the trees above them and landed in Honor's hair. Johnny picked it out of her blond tresses and was about to toss it aside when Honor gasped.

"No, let me," she said, taking it from him. She waited for a gust of wind and released the leaf, watching it catch the currents and soar, free and trembling, off on a great adventure.

Tears sparkled in her eyes as she turned back to Johnny. "That was your grandfather wishing us good luck."

Epilogue

Six Months Later . . .

Johnny had never seen the river look like that. Even in his youth, when the sunsets had often been spectacular, he'd never seen the twilight sky open up and pour out its fire, turning the water's surface to a necklace of dark jewels set in gold.

The crowd that had gathered for the ceremony alongside the riverbanks seemed silenced by its beauty. Or perhaps it was the woman walking among them who created the hush. The water's jeweled surface was Honor's backdrop as she approached the canopy of cottonwoods where Johnny stood with Chy Starhawk. In her fringed and beaded buckskin dress and with her hair around her shoulders, she looked as if she'd risen from the river's golden radiance.

"Johnny," she said, his name on her lips even before she'd reached him. Tears sparkled in her eyes as if she were reliving some tender moment of their adolescence. She came to stand beside him and took his dusky hand, reminding him how different they were, and how much the same.

Johnny thought about the gamut of emotion he'd

experienced in their relationship—the young love and reverence, the hurt, the hatred, the grief—and realized he'd come full circle. Perhaps he could never love her with the same fierce purity of youth, perhaps their innocence was gone forever, but the reverence was there, the sweetness that ripped through his heart and seared his soul like fire. His feelings for her were as deep and spiritual as they were animal. They'd taken on a unifying force that seemed as elemental as the earth itself.

Their hands joined, they turned to face Chy Starhawk and to silently receive his blessings. In the ancient language of the Apache, the shaman said a traditional prayer for the woman first, and then for the man, after which he turned in each direction of the compass, offering sacred pollen to the four winds.

When he was finished, Chy Starhawk stepped aside, and the minister of the church Honor had attended as a child stepped forward. "We are gathered here today to unite this man and this woman in holy matrimony," he said to the crowd.

Blood roared through Johnny's heart, blocking out everything else the clergyman said. Johnny heard nothing but the low thunder of the river behind them, the answering thunder of his pulse. He was aware that Honor had released his hand, that she was standing beside him, but nothing else reached his consciousness until the minister repeated the phrase, "Who gives this woman . . . ?"

In the silence that followed, Johnny turned to the crowd and saw Hale Bartholomew rise. The older man's blue eyes were lit like torches in the frail bones of his face. They burned with the pride of his bearing and the last vestiges of his indomitable will to win. Honor's father was reluctant in his surrender, but Johnny accepted the grace with which the older man met his gaze, the wisdom with which he acknowledged what was inevitable. They might never be friends, Johnny realized, but they both loved the same woman, and that would keep them from being enemies, from meeting in the battleground of the courtroom.

"I do," Hale Bartholomew said. "I give this woman." Johnny watched as Honor's eyes filled with tears. He wanted to stop the ceremony and take her into his arms. He wanted to shield her from anything and everything that could hurt her, but he knew her pain came from joy. She hadn't expected her father to come to this ceremony, or that he would ever dignify their union in such a way.

Johnny reached for her hand, gripping it tightly. As they turned back to the minister, something that might have been tears blurred his own eyes. He felt her joy, her pain. He wanted her to feel his reassurance. It would be all right. They would balance the years of heartbreak with as many years of happiness. Only tears of joy, Honor, he promised silently, swearing to do everything in his power to keep that vow. Only tears of joy.

The crowd rose to their feet as the minister pronounced the couple husband and wife. As Johnny turned to Honor, he caught a glimpse of familiar faces among the guests—Chase Beaudine with a cowboy hat tilted low over his eyes and a dimpled redheaded baby in his arms. His wife, Annie, was standing next to him, very proud, very pregnant. Even Geoff Dias was there, sitting on his Harley at the back of the assembly, a raffish smile on his face. But what Johnny didn't see as he bent to kiss his new bride was the hawk soaring over their heads.

It swooped and dipped above them, its snow-white wingtips silvery in the sunlight as it pulled out of a graceful dive and swept upward, ever upward, rising to meet the falling sun. Chy Starhawk saw the magnificent creature and turned, following the bird's ascent until, in a sudden, brilliant flash, it disappeared from sight. It was a good omen. All things would flow in harmony for the new couple, the sun, the moon, the stars. Their love, brought to life at the river's edge, would be fruitful, just as the spring floods made the earth warm and the soil fertile. The seed of their seed would be favored for generations to come.

The shaman smiled. His blessing had been heard.

THE EDITOR'S CORNER

Soon we'll be rushing into the holiday season, and we have some special LOVESWEPT books to bring you good cheer. Nothing can put you in a merrier mood than the six fabulous romances coming your way next month.

The first book in our lineup is **PRIVATE LESSONS** by Barbara Boswell, LOVESWEPT #582. Biology teacher Gray McCall remembers the high school student who'd had a crush on him, but now Elissa Emory is all grown up and quite a knockout. Since losing his family years ago, he hadn't teased or flirted with a woman, but he can't resist when Elissa challenges him to a sizzling duel of heated embraces and fiery kisses. Extracurricular activity has never been as tempting as it is in Barbara's vibrantly written romance.

With **THE EDGE OF PARADISE,** LOVESWEPT #583, Peggy Webb will tug at your heartstrings—and her hero will capture your heart. David Kelly is a loner, a man on the run who's come looking for sanctuary in a quiet Southern town. Still, he can't hide his curiosity—or yearning—for the lovely woman who lives next door. When he feels the ecstasy of being in Rosalie Brown's arms, he begins to wonder if he has left trouble behind and finally found paradise. A superb love story from Peggy!

Only Jan Hudson can come up with a heroine whose ability to accurately predict the weather stems from her once having been struck by lightning! And you can read all about it in **SUNNY SAYS,** LOVESWEPT #584. Kale Hoaglin is skeptical of Sunny Larkin's talent, and that's a problem since he's the new owner of the small TV station where Sunny works as the weather reporter. But her unerring predictions—and thrilling kisses—soon make a believer of him. Jan continues to delight with her special blend of love and laughter.

Please give a rousing welcome to new author Deborah Harmse and her first novel, **A MAN TO BELIEVE IN**, LOVESWEPT #585. This terrific story begins when Cori McLaughlin attends a costume party and catches the eye of a wickedly good-looking pirate. Jake Tanner can mesmerize any woman, and Cori's determined not to fall under his spell. But to be the man in her life, Jake is ready to woo her with patience, persistence, and passion. Enjoy one of our New Faces of 1992!

Michael Knight feels as if he's been **STRUCK BY LIGHTNING** when he first sees Cassidy Harrold, in LOVESWEPT #586 by Patt Bucheister. A mysterious plot of his matchmaking father brought him to England, and with one glimpse of Cassidy, he knows he'll be staying around for a while. Cassidy has always had a secret yen for handsome cowboys, and tangling with the ex–rodeo star is wildly exciting, but can she be reckless enough to leave London behind for his Montana home? Don't miss this enthralling story from Patt!

Tonya Wood returns to LOVESWEPT with **SNEAK**, #587, and this wonderful romance has definitely been worth waiting for. When Nicki Sharman attacks the intruder in her apartment, she thinks he's an infamous cat burglar. But he turns out to be Val Santisi, the rowdy bad boy she's adored since childhood. He's working undercover to chase a jewel thief, and together they solve the mystery of who's robbing the rich—and steal each other's heart in the process. Welcome back, Tonya!

FANFARE presents four spectacular novels that are on sale this month. Ciji Ware, the acclaimed author of *Romantic Times* award-winner **ISLAND OF THE SWANS**, delivers

WICKED COMPANY, an engrossing love story set in London during the eighteenth century. As Sophie Mc-Gann moves through the fascinating—and bawdy—world of Drury Lane, she remains loyal to her dream . . . and the only man she has ever loved.

Trouble runs deep in **STILL WATERS,** a novel of gripping suspense and sensual romance by Tami Hoag, highly praised author of **LUCKY'S LADY.** When the body of a murder victim literally falls at Elizabeth Stuart's feet, she's branded a suspect. But Sheriff Dane Jantzen soon becomes convinced of her innocence, and together they must find the killer before another deadly strike can cost them their chance for love, even her very life.

In the grand tradition of **THORN BIRDS** comes **THE DREAMTIME LEGACY** by Norma Martyn, an epic novel of Australia and one unforgettable woman. Jenny Garnett is indomitable as she travels through life, from a childhood in a penal colony to her marriage to a mysterious aristocrat, from the harshness of aching poverty to the splendor of unthinkable riches.

Treat yourself to **MORE THAN FRIENDS,** the classic romance by bestselling author BJ James. In this charming novel, corporate magnate John Michael Bradford meets his match when he's rescued from a freak accident by diminutive beauty Jamie Brent. Mike always gets what he wants, and what he wants is Jamie. But growing up with six brothers has taught independent Jamie never to surrender to a man who insists on always being in control.

Also on sale this month in the hardcover edition from Doubleday is **LAST SUMMER** by Theresa Weir. The author of **FOREVER** has penned yet another passionate and emotionally moving tale, one that brings together a bad-boy actor and the beautiful widow who tames his heart.

The Delaneys are coming next month from FANFARE! This legendary family's saga continues with **THE DELANEY CHRISTMAS CAROL,** three original and sparkling novellas by none other than Iris Johansen, Kay Hooper, and Fayrene Preston. Read about three generations of Delaneys in love and the changing faces of Christmas past, present, and future—only from FANFARE.

Happy reading!

With best wishes,

Nita Taublib

Nita Taublib
Associate Publisher
LOVESWEPT and FANFARE

Don't miss these fabulous Bantam Fanfare
titles on sale in OCTOBER.

WICKED COMPANY
by Ciji Ware

STILL WATERS
by Tami Hoag

THE DREAMTIME LEGACY
by Norma Martyn

MORE THAN FRIENDS
by BJ James

And in hardcover from Doubleday,
LAST SUMMER
by Theresa Weir

WICKED COMPANY
by Ciji Ware
the bestselling author of
ISLAND OF THE SWANS

Eighteenth-century Scotland is a man's world, and a woman has few rights. But when Sophie McGann's father dies in prison after angering a powerful aristocrat, Sophie learns to fight for herself. Looking for a new start, she takes on the glorious and bawdy world of London's Drury Lane in the golden age of British theatre. There she becomes a favorite of the brilliant theatre manager David Garrick, who encourages Sophie's skill as a playwright. But Sophie also attracts the attention of dangerous men: a rigid censor who can destroy her career; a charming young wastrel who will try to maneuver her into marriage; an enigmatic nobleman who wants to possess her. Through it all Sophie remains loyal to the writer's fire that burns within her, and to the only man she loves, the Scottish actor Hunter Robertson—even when all she holds dear is at risk.

STILL WATERS
by Tami Hoag
"A master of the genre" —*Publisher's Weekly*

"Tami Hoag belongs at the top of everyone's favorite author list."
—*Romantic Times*

**A sizzling novel of romantic suspense by the author of
LUCKY'S LADY.**

All Elizabeth Stuart wants is a chance to reclaim her peace of mind—to escape the memories of a painful divorce. But she quickly discovers that in a small town called Still Creek, trouble is around every bend. For one day a murder victim literally falls at her feet, branding her a suspect and bringing her under the searching gaze of local sheriff Dane Jantzen. In the following scene, which begins at the site of the crime, Dane has all but accused her of the murder, and Elizabeth is having more than a little trouble restraining her temper. . . .

"At a loss for words, Ms. Stuart?" he asked softly, arching a mocking brow.

"No," she said through clenched teeth, her furious gaze fastening to the open neck of his black polo shirt because she didn't think she could look him in the eye without losing her temper altogether. "I just can't seem to find one bad enough to call you."

"There's a thesaurus on my desk. Feel free to use it."

"Don't tempt me, sugar," she said, lifting her chin and fixing him with a glare as she took a step back toward the waiting deputy. "What I'd like to do with it wouldn't exactly be good for the binding."

Dane chuckled in spite of the fact that he disliked her. She had a lot of sass . . . and a backside that could make a man's palms sweat, he observed as she sauntered away with Ellstrom. The way she filled out a pair of jeans was enough to make Levi Strauss rise from the dead. He felt his own body stir in response and he frowned.

It was too damn bad there was a chance she was a killer.

"You had better wait in the sheriff's office." The dispatcher hustled her into the office, thrust a Styrofoam cup of black coffee into her hand and bolted for her station, swinging the door shut behind her. That effectively cut the noise level erupting in the room beyond to a dull buzz, enclosing Elizabeth in a cocoon of peace.

To distract herself, she began a tour of the sheriff's office, studying, looking for clues about the man. Not that she cared on a personal level, she reminded herself. From what she'd seen, Dane Jantzen was a Grade A bastard. It was just good sense to know your adversary. She'd learned that lesson the hard way, underestimating her ex-husband's power and ruthlessness. Besides, she wanted every detail she could get for her story. She was a journalist now, albeit at a podunk weekly newspaper in

Middle of Nowhere, Minnesota, but a journalist nevertheless, and she was determined to do the job right.

She glanced around the office. There was nothing here of Dane Jantzen the man, no mounted deer heads or bowling trophies.

He was neat. Not a good sign. Men who were neat liked to be in control of everything and everyone around them. Dane Jantzen's desk shouted control. Files were labeled, stacked, and lined up just so. His blotter was spotless. His pens were all in their little ceramic holder, tips down.

Beside the telephone was the one personal item in the room— a small wooden picture frame. Dangling her cigarette from her lip, Elizabeth lifted the frame and turned it for a look. The photograph was of a young girl, perhaps ten or eleven, just showing signs of growing into gangly youth. Dressed in baggy shorts and a blazing orange T-shirt, she stood on a lawn somewhere holding up a sign done in multi-colored Magic Markers that read "I love you, Daddy."

Elizabeth felt a jolt of surprise and something else. *Daddy*. She took a drag on her cigarette and exhaled a jet stream of blue smoke as she returned the picture to its place.

"Jesus," she muttered. "Someone actually married the son of a bitch."

"She has since seen the error of her ways, I assure you," Dane said dryly.

Elizabeth whirled, managing to look guilty and knock her coffee to the floor all at once.

"Shit! I'm sorry."

He stuck his head out into the hall and calmly called to the dispatcher. "Lorraine, could we get a couple of towels in here, please?"

"I was looking for an ashtray," Elizabeth said, not quite able to meet Jantzen's steady gaze. She stooped down and grabbed the cup, dabbing ineffectually at the stain on the rug with a wadded-up Kleenex she'd fished out of the pocket of her jeans.

"I don't smoke." He hitched at his jeans and hunkered down in front of her. "It's not good for you."

Elizabeth forced a wry laugh, dousing the stub of her cigarette in what coffee was left in the cup. "What is these days besides oat bran and abstinence?"

"Telling the truth, for starters," Dane said placidly.

She lifted her head and sucked in a gulp of air, startled by his nearness. He was staring at her with those cool unblinking blue eyes. The corners of the sensually curved mouth curled up slightly in that predatory way. He made no move to touch her, but she could feel him just the same. He was too close.

Instinctively she leaned back, but her fanny hit the front of his desk and she realized he had her trapped. It wasn't a pleasant sensation. Neither was the strange racing of her heart. This was hardly the time for her hormones to kick in. Fighting the feelings, she lifted her stubborn chin and looked him in the eye.

"Telling the truth is my business, sheriff."

"Really? I thought you were a reporter."

The gray eyes flashed like lightning behind storm clouds. Dane smiled a little wider and leaned a little closer, driven to recklessness by something he didn't quite understand. He enjoyed baiting her. He put the rush down to the excitement of the game, even though deep down he knew there were sexual connotations that had certainly been missing when he'd relished a win on the football field. This was a different kind of game. Elizabeth Stuart was a beautiful woman. He wasn't stupid enough to get involved with her, but that didn't mean he couldn't skirt the edges a little bit. It was like teasing an animal in a cage—he was safe just as long as he stayed back far enough to keep from getting bitten.

At that thought, his gaze drifted to her mouth. Cherry red. Cherry ripe. Too damn close.

"Your towels, sheriff."

Lorraine's stern, disapproving voice broke the sexual tension. Dane pushed himself to his feet and took the terry cloths the dispatcher thrust at him.

"Thank you, Lorraine."

"I've told those people out there you have nothing further to say, but they aren't leaving. Apparently they're waiting for *her*," she said, stabbing Elizabeth with a pointed look.

Elizabeth rose on shaky legs, setting aside the coffee cup with one hand and raking back her wild black mane with the other. "I won't have anything to say to them."

"Have Ellstrom roust them out of here," Dane said. "They can wait in the parking lot."

The secretary nodded and went to do his bidding. Dane dropped the towels to the wet spot on the floor and stepped on them with the toe of his sneaker. He glanced up at Elizabeth from beneath his eyelashes.

"Is your refusal to talk to them just professional courtesy or are you more concerned about the anything-you-say-can-and-will-be-used-against-you-in-a-court-of-law thing?"

"Why should I be worried about that? You haven't charged me with anything. Or is that your cute little way of telling me you've decided I killed Jarvis, then obligingly called 911? Please, Sheriff, I hope I don't look that stupid."

"Naw . . . stupid isn't how you look at all," he drawled, sliding into the chair behind his desk. He let his gaze glide down her, from the top of her tousled head down to the wet spot on the knee of her tight jeans where the coffee had got her on its way to the floor.

He was being an asshole and he knew it, but he couldn't seem to help himself. Elizabeth Stuart was just the kind of woman who brought out the bastard in him—beautiful, ambitious, greedy, willing to use herself to get what she wanted, willing to use anyone she knew. His gaze drifted back up and lingered on the swell of her breasts.

"Christ, you ought to about have it all memorized by now, hadn't you?" Elizabeth snapped, dropping her hands to her hips. It unnerved her to have him look at her that way. It unnerved her even more to feel excitement sparking to life inside her. It made her wonder if her body didn't just have fatally bad judgment in men. This one was six lanky feet of trouble, and logically she knew better than to get within scratching distance of him, but logic couldn't explain the heat his gaze inspired, nor could it dispel the disappointment she felt in herself for being attracted to him.

He didn't apologize for his rudeness. She doubted he ever apologized for anything. He nodded toward the visitor's chair in a silent order for her to sit, the gesture once again reminding her of a Nordic prince. He sat in his desk chair with a kind of negligent grace, staring at her with his brooding blue eyes. Jantzen didn't seem a particularly Scandinavian name. The Z made her think it was probably Slavic. But the blood was there somewhere, maybe on his mother's side—if he had one, she added uncharitably. The sleek blond hair, the high broad forehead, the heavy brow, the unyielding jaw, those cool, cool eyes all spoke of some kinship with the Vikings.

He nodded again toward the chair. "Have a seat, Mrs. Stuart."

"Miss," she corrected him, moving her camera from the chair to a stack of files on the desk. She settled herself on the chair and pulled her purse onto her lap to hunt for another cigarette.

"You dropped the Mrs., but kept the last name. Is that proper?"

"I don't really give a damn."

"I suppose by that point in time you'd probably lost track of what name to go back to anyway."

That wasn't true, but Elizabeth didn't tell Dane Jantzen. Her roots went back to West Texas, scenic rock and rattlesnake country, to a cowboy named J.C. Shelby and a mother who had died before Elizabeth could store any memories of her. But that was all too personal to reveal to this man.

Under the cynical hide she had grown over the years there was too much vulnerability. She seldom acknowledged it, but she knew it was there. She would have to be a fool to reveal it to this man, and she had ceased being a fool some time ago. So she let Dane Jantzen think what he wanted and told herself his sarcasm couldn't hurt her.

"I can see where you might have felt you didn't get anything out of him in the divorce so you might as well try to wring a few bucks out of his name," Jantzen said, steepling his long fingers in front of him. "That's just business as usual for you, right?"

"I kept the name because my son didn't need another change in his life," she said, her cool snapping like a dry twig beneath the weight of the sheriff's taunt. She leaned forward on her chair, poised for battle, shaking her cigarette at him. "He didn't need another reminder that Brock Stuart didn't want him."

And neither did I.

The words hung in the air between them, unspoken but adding to the thick emotional tension. Dane sat back, a little shaken, a little ashamed of himself, not at all pleased that his poking had stripped away a layer of armor and given him a glimpse of the woman behind it. The truth was he didn't want

Elizabeth Stuart to be anything other than what he had preconceived her to be—a cold, calculating, manipulative gold digger.

Elizabeth sat back, forcing her stiff shoulders against the chair, a little shaken, a lot afraid that she had just revealed a weakness. What had happened to her restraint? What had happened to that hard-earned thick skin? The stress of the evening was wearing on her. And Dane Jantzen was wearing on her. To cover her blunder she turned the cigarette in her hand, planted it between her lips and lit it as quickly as she could so as not to let Jantzen see her hands shake.

"I'd rather you didn't smoke," he said.

"And I'd rather you weren't a jerk." She deliberately took a deep pull on the cigarette, presented him with her profile and fired a stream of smoke into the air, looking askance at him. "Looks like neither one of us is going to get our wish."

Dane yanked open a desk drawer, pulled out a black plastic ashtray and tossed it across the desk in her general direction.

Elizabeth arched a brow. "What a gentleman."

"You ought to see what they taught me in charm school."

THE DREAMTIME LEGACY
by bestselling Australian author
Norma Martyn

In the tradition of THE THORN BIRDS, THE DREAMTIME LEGACY is a magnificent, epic novel of Australia and the unforgettable woman who tames this harsh, beautiful land and makes it her own.

From her childhood in the gutters of an Aussie penal colony to her marriage at the age of eleven to a mysterious English aristocrat, from aching poverty to unimaginable riches, Jenny Garnett is a woman of indomitable strength and courage. Set against the fascinating, exotic, little-known heart of Australia, THE DREAMTIME LEGACY brings to life the legendary outback—and a heroine as fiery as Scarlett O'Hara.

Travis was waiting for Jenny when she left the tavern.

She glanced at him, her eyes narrowing, and began to run toward the waterfront lodgings of the serving girls.

"Wait!" he called to her. "You have no need to run away. I merely wish to speak with you."

She paused, turning toward him, watching him approach.

"What do you want to talk to me about?"

When he asked her to marry him, she stared at him, eyes again wary.

"Don't you trust me?" he asked, studying her in the light of the oil lamps along the waterfront.

"You're crazed," she said slowly, still watching him cautiously, her hands beginning to curl into two balled fists, readying to protect her.

"Do I look crazed?"

"No. But you talk crazed."

"Because I asked you to marry me?" When she did not reply, he continued patiently, "I came to Sydney to find a wife. When I saw you, I decided you would fill the role quite adequately. What I mean is, I decided you would fill the bill. Do you understand?"

She stared at him a moment longer, then nodded.

"Well now. We're making progress," Travis said. "In this Colony it's not unusual for a man to visit Sydney to select a wife from among the women he notices, is it?"

"I don't know."

"How long have you been in the Colony?"

"Always."

"Then you must know," he said, impatience edging into his voice. "It's common practice here. It happens all the time."

"Not to me, it doesn't!" Jenny retorted, responding to the changed tone of his voice.

"You're not already married, are you?" he asked.

She laughed then, and shook her head.

"Do you have parents I should consult? Your mother or your father?"

"My mother's dead." She frowned, then added, "My father's gone too."

A thought occurred to Travis. "Are you an indentured servant in the tavern? A convict?"

She shook her head again.

"Then you're quite free?"

She nodded, remembering the birds, and she smiled at him for the first time.

"That's better. You're not very talkative . . . an advantage in the wife a man chooses."

"Did you really choose me?" she asked. "You weren't just talking crazed? Or funning me?"

"I don't have time to make sport of finding a wife," he replied shortly. "I want to leave the Colony tomorrow. I need to return home." He paused for a moment, looking out toward the headlands and the open ocean beyond. "We have a long journey south and we need to complete the journey before the early snows arrive."

"Snow?" Jenny looked at him, her eyes widening. "I've never seen snow. But I know what snow is." She smiled at him again, a show of pride in her expression reflecting the spirit he had detected earlier. "I can read and write. Now I'm up to reading a book. A whole book! That's how I learned about snow."

"You'll learn more about it where we're going."

"Where are you taking me?"

"A long way. High up into the Australian alps. To a valley there."

"Are there birds where you're taking me?"

"Many birds. And many animals too."

"I'd like to go with you if there are birds there."

"Then that's settled. We can be married tonight," he told her. "I've already made the arrangements."

Everything in its proper order, he thought. Back to front and upside down, like the country he now chose to call home. First the saddle ordered, then the mare selected. First the preacher arranged, then the wife selected.

He stared at the harbor for a while, then toward the open ocean beyond.

The girl watched him, a somber older wisdom slowly shadowing her young face.

"You're an English gentleman," she said finally. "I can tell by the way you talk. Not from the things you say but by the way you say them." There was the beginning of retreat in her voice, and of regret on her face. "You chose me 'cause you thought I was a respectable serving wench. But I'm convict blood, mother and father both. You asked me about them but I didn't properly tell you. My mother was a half-starved foundling to begin with and a thief and a whore all her life. And I've no way of knowing who my father was, though she did say he was likely one of two, either a Cockney cut-throat who got himself hanged before I was born or one of the Irish rebels she spent a spell with. I've always felt in myself it was an Irish convict and not the other one."

She was watching him as she spoke. When he turned to look at her, her determination faltered.

"You're talkative when you choose to be," he said.

"I'm a good girl for all my bad blood," she told him then. "But it's best you know all that, so you can have second thoughts."

She waited for him to speak—a brown-haired waif with merry green eyes that had become serious, asking for nothing, expecting nothing.

"One of these days, when we've been married for a while and we know each other better, I may tell you about myself," Travis said.

One of these days. But he knew he never would. And he felt certain he would never be questioned by Jenny Garnett.

He no longer questioned himself. There came a time when a man couldn't stomach the half-truths he told others; even less the half-truths he told himself. Then he shut a door on questions and answers, and built whatever he could on whatever was left.

"There's one thing I think you should tell me about yourself before then," Jenny said.

Her words cut so sharply across his thoughts, he glared at her.

"What do you feel you have a right to know?" he demanded, his tone rough and harsh.

"Just one thing, sir. What's your name?"

Travis burst into laughter, a strident sound abrasive to his own ears.

"Jonathan Travis," he told her; and he laughed again at the bitter half-truth even in that.

MORE THAN FRIENDS
by BJ James

"For sheer emotional intensity, no one surpasses the marvelously gifted BJ James." —*Romantic Times*

A charming romance by bestselling BJ James about a beautiful former Olympic hopeful who becomes entangled with a powerful corporate magnate.

From the moment she saved his life, Jamie Brent's peaceful world was shattered by the presence of handsome business tycoon Mike Bradford. Suddenly her every step was dogged by media hounds, wild rumors of a heated love affair filled the daily tabloids, and Bradford had moved into her life with all the subtlety of a corporate takeover. Worst of all, Jamie feared she was falling victim to the magic Bradford was so adept at weaving, leaving her heart vulnerable once more . . .

His hands stopped their stroking and untangled from her hair to frame her face. Slowly his head descended to hers. There was no urgency, no deep, frantic need, only the sweet kiss of promise. When he lifted his lips from hers, Jamie could only think of this moment, this instant. There were no frustrations, no anger, no troublesome reporters, and no disillusioning mistakes in the past. There was only Mike.

Because of her intense training schedule, Jamie had never learned to hide her response behind a cloak of flirtatiousness. Those teen years when most girls were perfecting the art, she had spent perfecting her gymnastics skills. She had never been anything but straightforward and totally honest. That beguiling truthfulness was a window to her heart.

She feared the experienced man who was now towering over her could read every thought that was sure to be written on her expressive face. Even now he was watching her silently, holding her gently, as she ran the gamut from elation to panic. Despite her efforts at control, her delicate brows arched up in wonder, her sapphire eyes sparkled in excitement, the soft and tender curve of her lips trembled on the brink of a smile. Then, just as swiftly, the smile faded, even as it was born. A shiver passed through her as a shutter came down over the glow in her face. Instantly her guard was up. She could feel his piercing gaze as she struggled valiantly to gather her scattered thoughts, to become again the coolly aloof Jamie. Jamie, who cloaked herself in aloneness. Now she felt the small crack that had appeared in her wall of defense, and she must begin to mend it, while she still could. The battle he had predicted had begun, and Jamie knew she was fighting herself as well as Mike.

Wisely he put her from him. The faintly mocking smile that marked his face was for himself, not the sweet innocent who could devastate him with her eyes. When he spoke, there was no mockery or teasing, only gentle caring.

"Tonight, whether you admit it or not, that shield you've been hiding behind has cracked. I serve you fair warning: I'll use any means to keep the rift open until someday you help me tear it away."

"I won't."

"You will, but don't be frightened. I might not be fair, but I will be gentle, I will be patient, and I will win." He touched her cheek softly, his voice even huskier. "I've never before been a patient lover, but never before was there a Jamie Brent."

"This is impossible," she whispered.

"No, honey, it's inevitable."

Jamie shivered beneath his certainty. With her once gleaming eyes grown dark, she reached for the pins that had held her hair. She felt the need to control the tangled locks as she would her capricious emotions.

"No," he growled, capturing her hand in his as it hovered over the low table where he had dropped the pins. "Leave it down. I like it free."

"Very well, if you wish." She could feel his anger at her need to withdraw behind her wall of total control for it grated in his voice. With stilted gestures she used her free hand to push her hair back from her shoulders. It fell gloriously, shining and healthy, to her waist. "If you still insist we go out to dinner dressed as we are, I suggest we leave now."

"Jamie"—he caught her other hand—"don't shut me out. The woman who opened the door to me tonight was alive and full of joy. Don't lock her away. She'll die, honey. She'll die without ever having lived. Let her be free and as vibrantly alive as she can be. Don't twist all your emotions into a tight little knot until they wither and die." He wound a strand of hair around his hand. "Don't confine her hair, or her spirit. Be a woman. Entrance me, beguile me, tease me as you did tonight with those marvelous clothes. For a moment I saw a woman who could conquer the world with her smile.

"Come out from behind that protective cloak that has kept you an innocent." He paused at the harsh hiss of her indrawn breath. "No, don't deny it. In many ways you're the most innocent twenty-six-year-old woman I've ever seen. Innocent in the ways of women, innocent of your strength. Come into the real world, stand on your own two feet, ply your womanly wiles. Flaunt your charms, flex your wings, and learn the power you can wield. Jamie, Jamie, you could drive a man to the brink of madness."

"You're crazy. I can't do that. I wouldn't know how."

"Then learn, and begin with me. First, last, and always."

She watched his solemn face for a long while. "You're serious, aren't you?"

"Never more."

"I don't understand. Why should you bother? Why should you care?"

"It's simple. I want you to come to me as all the woman you can be. I want the fire and I want the excitement only you can give me. Ours could be an explosive relationship. We could share a matchless love, but only if each of us brings total commitment to our joining. I'm selfish, honey; I want it all. I want the woman in my life to love me without reservations—as I'll love her."

"Mike, you're going too fast for me. All the other was fun and games compared to this. I'm not ready for it. I'm not sure I'll ever be."

"I hadn't intended getting into this tonight. You're right, it's far too soon. Let's forget it for now. I'm still starved."

Jamie burst into hearty laughter that was tinged with relief. "I suppose giants do need to refuel with a certain regularity. Come, you poor man, let's go."

Though an easy rapport had been established, she was still wary and was likely to be for some time. But the crack was still there in the wall. It was a beginning.

OFFICIAL RULES TO WINNERS CLASSIC SWEEPSTAKES

No Purchase necessary. To enter the sweepstakes follow instructions found elsewhere in this offer. You can also enter the sweepstakes by hand printing your name, address, city, state and zip code on a 3" x 5" piece of paper and mailing it to: Winners Classic Sweepstakes, P.O. Box 785, Gibbstown, NJ 08027. Mail each entry separately. Sweepstakes begins 12/1/91. Entries must be received by 6/1/93. Some presentations of this sweepstakes may feature a deadline for the Early Bird prize. If the offer you receive does, then to be eligible for the Early Bird prize your entry must be received according to the Early Bird date specified. Not responsible for lost, late, damaged, misdirected, illegible or postage due mail. Mechanically reproduced entries are not eligible. All entries become property of the sponsor and will not be returned.

Prize Selection/Validations: Winners will be selected in random drawings on or about 7/30/93, by VENTURA ASSOCIATES, INC., an independent judging organization whose decisions are final. Odds of winning are determined by total number of entries received. Circulation of this sweepstakes is estimated not to exceed 200 million. Entrants need not be present to win. All prizes are guaranteed to be awarded and delivered to winners. Winners will be notified by mail and may be required to complete an affidavit of eligibility and release of liability which must be returned within 14 days of date of notification or alternate winners will be selected. Any guest of a trip winner will also be required to execute a release of liability. Any prize notification letter or any prize returned to a participating sponsor, Bantam Doubleday Dell Publishing Group, Inc., its participating divisions or subsidiaries, or VENTURA ASSOCIATES, INC. as undeliverable will be awarded to an alternate winner. Prizes are not transferable. No multiple prize winners except as may be necessary due to unavailability, in which case a prize of equal or greater value will be awarded. Prizes will be awarded approximately 90 days after the drawing. All taxes, automobile license and registration fees, if applicable, are the sole responsibility of the winners. Entry constitutes permission (except where prohibited) to use winners' names and likenesses for publicity purposes without further or other compensation.

Participation: This sweepstakes is open to residents of the United States and Canada, except for the province of Quebec. This sweepstakes is sponsored by Bantam Doubleday Dell Publishing Group, Inc. (BDD), 666 Fifth Avenue, New York, NY 10103. Versions of this sweepstakes with different graphics will be offered in conjunction with various solicitations or promotions by different subsidiaries and divisions of BDD. Employees and their families of BDD, its division, subsidiaries, advertising agencies, and VENTURA ASSOCIATES, INC., are not eligible.

Canadian residents, in order to win, must first correctly answer a time limited arithmetical skill testing question. Void in Quebec and wherever prohibited or restricted by law. Subject to all federal, state, local and provincial laws and regulations.

Prizes: The following values for prizes are determined by the manufacturers' suggested retail prices or by what these items are currently known to be selling for at the time this offer was published. Approximate retail values include handling and delivery of prizes. Estimated maximum retail value of prizes: 1 Grand Prize ($27,500 if merchandise or $25,000 Cash); 1 First Prize ($3,000); 5 Second Prizes ($400 each); 35 Third Prizes ($100 each); 1,000 Fourth Prizes ($9.00 each) ; 1 Early Bird Prize ($5,000); Total approximate maximum retail value is $50,000. Winners will have the option of selecting any prize offered at level won. Automobile winner must have a valid driver's license at the time the car is awarded. Trips are subject to space and departure availability. Certain black-out dates may apply. Travel must be completed within one year from the time the prize is awarded. Minors must be accompanied by an adult. Prizes won by minors will be awarded in the name of parent or legal guardian.

For a list of Major Prize Winners (available after 7/30/93): send a self-addressed, stamped envelope entirely separate from your entry to: Winners Classic Sweepstakes Winners, P.O. Box 825, Gibbstown, NJ 08027. Requests must be received by 6/1/93. DO NOT SEND ANY OTHER CORRESPONDENCE TO THIS P.O. BOX.

The Delaney Dynasty lives on in

The Delaney Christmas Carol

by Kay Hooper, Iris Johansen, & Fayrene Preston

Three of romantic fiction's best-loved authors present the changing face of Christmas spirit—past, present, and future—as they tell the story of three generations of Delaneys in love.

CHRISTMAS PAST by Iris Johansen

From the moment he first laid eyes on her, Kevin Delaney felt a curious attraction for the ragclad Gypsy beauty rummaging through the attic of his ranch at Killara. He didn't believe for a moment her talk of magic mirrors and second-sight, but something about Zara St. Cloud stirred his blood. Now, as Christmas draws near, a touch leads to a kiss and a gift of burning passion.

CHRISTMAS PRESENT by Fayrene Preston

Bria Delaney had been looking for Christmas ornaments in her mother's attic, when she saw him in the mirror for the first time—a stunningly handsome man with sky-blue eyes and red-gold hair. She had almost convinced herself he was only a dream when Kells Braxton arrived at Killara and led them both to a holiday wonderland of sensuous pleasure.

CHRISTMAS FUTURE by Kay Hooper

As the last of the Delaney men, Brett returned to Killara this Christmastime only to find it in the capable hands of his father's young and beautiful widow. Yet the closer he got to Cassie, the more Brett realized that the embers of their old love still burned and that all it would take was a look, a kiss, a caress, to turn their dormant passion into an inferno.

The best in Women's Fiction from Bantam FANFARE.
On sale in November 1992   AN 428 9/92